'Carlos, there's

But he was moving along the sofa with smooth, fluid, sexy movements of his muscular body. She waited as he took hold of her hands, tenderly caressing the palms until she could feel her resolution beginning to evaporate.

'Carlos…'

As he kissed her, she closed her eyes in absolute bliss, losing all the inhibitions she'd tried to fix firmly in place. But time was running out. She mustn't go on pretending that she was free to make love because…

'I'm pregnant!' She pulled herself away as she cried out.

Dear Reader

Ah, Rome! One of my favourite cities—and one of the most romantic! The atmosphere is electric, exciting, invigorating. It's a city where couples in love like to spend long, lazy weekends walking along the fascinating streets, visiting the awesome temples and palaces, perhaps lingering beside the Trevi Fountain before returning to some cosy hotel where romance is always on the menu.

DR FELLINI'S PREGNANT BRIDE is the first book in my Italian duo about twin English sisters, Sarah and Lucy, both doctors, who find themselves in the same Roman hospital, set beside the Tiber river, and fall in love amidst the energy of the Accident and Emergency department.

In the second book, Lucy finds love with the charismatic, divinely handsome Vittorio Vincenzi. They both have reason to feel cautious about falling in love, but are magnetically drawn to each other. Each of them has their own secrets—will their blossoming romance continue when they divulge those secrets to each other?

I hope you enjoy reading these two books as much as I have enjoyed writing them.

Margaret Barker

Read Lucy's story coming soon
from Mills & Boon® Medical Romance™

ROMAN HOSPITAL

The romance of Rome, the excitement of A&E!

DR FELLINI'S PREGNANT BRIDE

BY
MARGARET BARKER

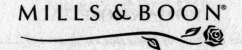

MILLS & BOON®

*First published in Great Britain 2004
Harlequin Mills & Boon Limited,
Eton House, 18-24 Paradise Road, Richmond, Surrey TW9 1SR*

© Margaret Barker 2004

ISBN 0 263 83910 9

*Set in Times Roman 10½ on 11½ pt.
03-0704-51153*

*Printed and bound in Spain
by Litografia Rosés, S.A., Barcelona*

CHAPTER ONE

THE plane swayed. Sarah clung to the washbasin to steady herself. How long had she been in this loo? A couple of minutes at most. That was all the time she dared spend here. All four lavatories at the back of the plane had been vacant when she'd arrived. She'd deliberately chosen the quiet time when everyone had settled into their pre-lunch drinks whilst watching the film.

Sarah stared once more at the thin blue line on the plastic container. No doubt about it. She really was pregnant!

She couldn't hang around in here much longer. Any minute now someone would knock on the door. There might even be a call over the loudspeaker asking for Dr Sarah Montgomery. One of the perks of air travel was that she was upgraded to club class if she agreed to give medical help in an emergency.

Sarah tipped out the fluid from its container and stuffed everything else into her cabin bag. As she emerged into the cramped area around the toilet facilities, a large, motherly lady of indeterminate age was making her way down the aisle.

'You OK, dear?'

'I'm fine!' Sarah forced a smile to appear on her taut, dry lips.

The woman frowned. 'I wouldn't ask, only you look a bit peaky to me. Time of the month, is it?'

'Something like that.'

If only!

The woman folded her arms and prepared for a long chat to while away the journey time.

'Women's problems! Tell me about it. If men only knew how lucky they were! I'd change places any day with my husband. No periods, no pregnancies, no babies…'

'Absolutely! Well, if you'll excuse me, I'll get back to my seat.'

Sarah eased her way past the well-meaning lady and escaped to the safety of her seat near the front. She remembered being asked when she'd checked in if she would be prepared to help out in a medical emergency on the plane. The way she was feeling now, it seemed as if she was the medical emergency!

Get a grip, girl! It's not the end of the world. It may seem like it at the moment with your mind in a state of shock. All the implications of an unplanned pregnancy are crowding in on you but you'll work something out. When you've come to terms with this seemingly impossible situation! When your thoughts have stopped spinning around…

Sarah tried to calm herself as she stared out of the window. Below her the jagged peaks of the Alps were covered in snow. In London it had felt cold enough for snow but the streets had only suffered a light January drizzle as she'd boarded the airport express at the crack of dawn.

She'd been feeling queasy for the last few days, especially in the mornings. If she hadn't been so busy getting ready to leave the flat and finalise her work at the hospital she would have had more time to put two and two together. But this morning when she'd actually been sick, cold reality had set in. As soon as she'd checked in she'd made for the chemist's and bought herself a pregnancy testing kit.

'Would you like some champagne, madam?'

As Sarah brought the glass to her lips she remembered that this was how it had all started. One celebratory glass of champagne with her ex-boyfriend Robin. And then another one because they'd had a lot to celebrate, hadn't they?

It had been nearly Christmas and, more importantly, they'd both got new exciting jobs starting in the New Year. Robin had called round to pick up the rest of his stuff and had brought two bottles of champagne, one of them intended for the party he had been going to that evening.

The first bottle had soon been empty and Robin had suggested drinking the other. For old times' sake. It had been good while it had lasted, hadn't it? And there had been no hard feelings when they had decided to split up, had there?

No hard feelings, she'd agreed in her woozy state. They'd had some good times together. Coming home from the hospital when they'd both happened to be off duty together. Picking up a take-away and a video for a nice relaxing evening.

One of the best years of his life, Robin had said, but he was glad it was over so that he could go back to being single again. Neither of them had wanted a real lifelong commitment. They both wanted to travel the world, live every moment to the full.

It was at that point, she remembered, when Robin had been eulogising about the great big wide world out there, that he'd leaned across to give her a hug. And flushed with nostalgia, remembering only the good times, one thing had led to another... Oh, how could she have been so stupid as to end up in bed with Robin? They'd ruined a perfectly amicable ending to a relationship, resulting in her present complication.

Complication? It was a disaster!

She was starting a new job in Rome. If she had the baby, how long would she be able to keep working? Where would she raise the baby, Italy or England? She'd have to keep working as a single mum to support herself and her child. What about childcare when she was working?

And then there was Robin to think about! She'd have to tell Robin he was going to be a father. Robin a father! The idea was preposterous. But fathers had rights. He would have to be told. But supposing he suggested they get back together for the sake of the child. She'd been so relieved when their relationship had ended. They couldn't possibly start again with all the problems of a baby that neither of them had… But for the sake of the child, would she be prepared to…?

'Dr Montgomery?'

The stewardess was holding out the champagne bottle for a top-up. Sarah put her hand over her glass.

'No, thanks.'

Some sane part of her brain was telling her that too much champagne wouldn't be good for the baby. The baby! It was only a six-week embryo, for heaven's sake! But she put the glass down on the seat tray in front of her and placed her hands over her abdomen as if she was just resting them there. Her tummy felt normal. No sign that a new life was springing up there—yet.

'Excuse me, Dr Montgomery.'

'Yes?'

Sarah gathered her thoughts as she sat up straight in her seat and looked up at the stewardess who had offered her more champagne.

'A young girl's been taken ill at the back of the plane. She's finding it hard to breathe. Would you come and take a look at her?'

'Of course.'

Sarah's brain clicked in and her medical training took over as she followed the stewardess down the long aisle. The cabin crew had put some cushions and a blanket on the floor at the side of the galley so that the girl could lie down.

The child stared up at Sarah with terrified eyes as she struggled with her breathing. The stewardess had told Sarah that the girl was called Judy; she was eight years old and was travelling as an unaccompanied minor. All the cabin crew had been alerted to the fact that they must keep an eye on Judy because she didn't have an adult with her.

'Hello, Judy,' Sarah said, putting her arm around the girl and easing her into a sitting position. 'I'm Dr Sarah. Would you like to tell me how you're feeling?'

'I can't breathe,' Judy said, wheezing heavily. 'I can't get to the top of my breath. Do you know what I mean, Sarah?'

Sarah nodded. 'I know exactly what you mean, Judy. I've treated lots of patients like you. Have you had a problem with your breathing before?'

The young girl frowned. 'When I was six I had asthma but the doctor said it had gone into...into somewhere funny but I can't remember where.'

Sarah stroked the girl's dark hair, smoothing it back from her forehead. 'Your asthma went into remission, Judy, which simply means it went away. But sometimes it comes back, so I'm going to give you some oxygen to help your breathing get under control again.'

Sarah was checking through the emergency box that she'd asked the stewardess to bring. Different airlines had different first-aid systems. Most could usually provide oxygen. She knew she was in luck when she located the oxygen cylinder and mask.

'Judy, I'm just going to put this mask over your face and ask you to breathe as normally as you can. Will you do that for me?'

The young girl nodded, eyes still wide and frightened.

Sarah squeezed Judy's hand. 'This is really going to help you. That's right, just breathe gently. It's going to make you feel much better. I'll take it off any time you ask but if you can keep it on for a few minutes...'

Judy was saying something. Sarah lifted the mask to hear the request.

'Don't leave me, Sarah, will you?'

'No, of course I won't leave you,' Sarah said gently.

Sarah crouched on the floor of the plane, leaning her back against the cool plastic wall. Her own troubles had ceased to be of any consequence. That was the good thing about being in the medical profession. You could be in the middle of your own personal crisis and then suddenly you were called upon to deal with somebody who was really suffering and your own problems were put into perspective.

She glanced down at her patient. Judy's pulse was still too rapid but her breathing was settling down. Sarah removed the mask from the child's face.

Judy managed a smile. 'Thanks a lot, Sarah. I'm feeling a lot better now but I don't want to go back to my seat. The lady sitting in front of me is really horrid. She turned round when I first got on the plane and told me to stop kicking her seat. I hadn't kicked her seat, honestly! I was just trying to get the magazines out of the back of the pocket at the back of her seat and...'

Tears were welling and Judy's breathing was beginning to deteriorate again. Sarah put her arm around the little girl and helped her to her feet.

'Come and sit beside me. There's a spare seat next to me and nobody will be in front of you. You can stretch out your legs as much as you like.'

Sarah looked enquiringly at the stewardess as she took Judy back into club class. 'I don't want to leave my patient at the back of the plane,' she explained.

'Of course you don't, Doctor. Thank you very much for helping out. Judy's a much better colour now.'

'Yes, she's recovered well,' Sarah said, settling her charge into the big seat beside her. 'Could you bring her a drink, please?'

Judy was smiling now. Sarah realised that the young girl

was actually enjoying all the attention. She was expensively clothed in good-quality trousers and sweater, her hair neatly cut.

Sarah had formed the opinion that Judy's asthma attack had been brought on by the stress of setting out on an air journey by herself. It could be a scary ordeal for a young girl.

'Who's going to meet you when you get to Rome, Judy?' Sarah asked as the child sipped happily on her orange juice and nibbled a biscuit.

'My dad. He's Italian.'

That would account for the lovely dark hair, brown eyes and olive skin. Judy was very pretty now but she would be stunningly beautiful in a few years.

'And your mother?'

Judy put down her glass and turned to look at Sarah. 'Mum's on her honeymoon with James. They're English. We live in London. James has been living in our house since I was a baby. Mum's having another baby and she told James she wanted him to marry her. James said, what was the point. They were OK as they were. But Mum went on and on and…you wouldn't believe what they said to each other. One night they were having this big row and—'

'Perhaps you shouldn't tell me all this, Judy.'

Judy shrugged. 'Oh, it's OK. Everybody knows they had a big row and split up for a while. It was in the papers because James is quite famous.'

Judy mentioned the name of the character that James played in a soap opera, and Sarah nodded, remembering the gossip magazine she'd read at the hairdresser's. Poor little scrap, having to witness all this when she was only eight. No wonder the poor child's asthma had returned.

'I wanted to go on honeymoon with them. I've never been on a honeymoon,' Judy said solemnly. 'But James said…' Judy lowered her voice to a gruff whisper. 'Over his dead body. That I should go back to my dad. It's about time he—'

'I'll stay with you until you meet your father,' Sarah said quickly. 'I'd like to make sure he takes you to see a doctor while you're in Rome. How long do you think you'll be staying with your dad?'

Judy shrugged again. 'For ever if James gets his own way. He doesn't like me.'

Sarah swallowed hard as she reached over to squeeze Judy's hand.

'You'll enjoy being with your dad.'

'I hope so,' was the quiet response.

Judy's eyelids were drooping. Sarah tucked a blanket around her as the child drifted off to sleep. She felt like sleeping herself but her mind was too active. As soon as she stopped worrying about Judy her own problems crowded in again. She wondered, fleetingly, if Carlos would be at the airport to meet her. He'd e-mailed only yesterday to say that he'd try to make it. She'd told him it wasn't necessary, but if she knew Carlos he would be there unless there was some major disaster affecting the A and E department where he was consultant in charge.

She leaned back in her seat, remembering what a good friend he'd always been. As a child, when her family had taken her to the coast, south-west of Rome, and had rented the Villa Florissa overlooking the sea, which was owned by Carlos's father, she'd been delighted that Carlos, nine years older than herself, hadn't been bossy. He'd always been sympathetic and helpful with her when her mother had asked him to keep an eye on her and her twin Lucy.

And over the years the two families had kept in contact. So, when Carlos had written to say that he'd been appointed medical director of the A and E department of a large new hospital near the River Tiber in Rome, it had set her thinking about the possibility of making a move. Because of the

large number of tourists visiting Rome, Carlos had said that
the hospital was keen to recruit English-speaking doctors
for its A and E department.

Twenty-nine years old, Sarah had been enjoying her
work in London but, with her thirtieth birthday only a few
months away, she was feeling in need of a change.

She and Robin had been thinking about splitting up.
There hadn't seemed much point in staying together any
more and she had felt she had been at a crossroads in her
life. She had been working all day, spending her off-duty
time with the same group of friends from the hospital.
She'd always found travel to be stimulating and Rome, with
the stunningly beautiful areas surrounding it, was her favourite place in all the world.

Around the same time that Robin had applied to a French
medical-aid group in Africa, Sarah had contacted Carlos to
enquire about the possibility of working in Rome. Carlos
had arranged an interview for her in London and she'd been
accepted to work in his department. He'd told her over the
phone that he'd made a strong recommendation that she
should be accepted.

But nobody had foreseen that Sarah would have fallen
pregnant! Should she tell Carlos as soon as she met him so
that he could cancel her contract and find someone else?
Would that be the most honest course of action? After all,
she didn't want to become a liability after Carlos had given
her such a glowing character reference. But lots of women
worked through their pregnancies without being liabilities,
didn't they?

And she really, really wanted this job! She wanted the
chance to live in Rome, to visit all the places she'd loved
as a child and a teenager. She couldn't give all that up just
because…

The captain's voice over the loudspeaker interrupted her

thoughts. Apparently they were making their descent to Fiumicino airport and should fasten their seat belts.

Sarah gently removed the blanket from Judy and explained what was happening. The stewardess came round to check seat belts and leaned across to speak to Sarah and Judy.

'We've received a message that Judy's father will be two hours late at the airport. An important business meeting or something. He's requested the airport authorities to assign a ground stewardess to meet Judy off the plane and stay with her until he arrives so that—'

'No!' Judy's startled exclamation rang out over the sound of the engines. 'I want to stay with Sarah.'

'Don't worry, Judy,' Sarah said, holding the girl's hand tightly. 'I'll stay with you and the lady who's been asked to look after you until your father arrives.'

The stewardess smiled. 'Thank you so much, Doctor, for all your help.'

Sarah smiled back. What did another minor problem matter in her problematic day? She would have to explain to Carlos that she couldn't leave Judy until her father arrived. She would suggest that Carlos go back to hospital and she would follow later in a taxi.

'There he is! That's the doctor I told you about, Judy,' Sarah said as they emerged through customs to be greeted by the dark-haired, smiling Carlos.

The uniformed ground stewardess assigned to take charge of Judy stood to one side as the introductions were made.

'*Ciao*, Sarah. And who's this charming young *signorina*?' Carlos said, after giving Sarah a light friendly kiss on both cheeks.

'I'm Judy Mendicci. The airport lady is looking after me until my daddy can get here. He's going to be two hours late. Sarah is going to stay with me as well. I've got asthma and Sarah cured me on the plane.'

'Mendicci?' Carlos said thoughtfully. 'Tell me about your father, Judy. Where does he live?'

Judy thought for a moment. 'In a street just off the Via Veneto.'

Carlos nodded. 'Is your father Pietro Mendicci, by any chance?'

Judy looked surprised. 'Yes, do you know him?'

'Your father is very well known here in Rome. He's an extremely generous man, Judy. I've met Pietro on several occasions when he's made donations to our medical work. I'll give him a call and ask him to pick you up from the hospital. Two hours is a long time for you to wait here. Would you like that, Judy?'

'Oh, yes, please!'

When she had been growing up, it had never ceased to amaze Sarah how efficient Carlos could be. A problem arose and he solved it, effortlessly. Nothing ever fazed him. That was probably one of the reasons why he was so good at his job. It crossed her mind that he would be an ideal person to discuss her problem with. But not just yet! No need to spoil their reunion.

Carlos was making his phone call now, chatting amicably to Judy's father. The Italian words flowing from his tongue were like music to Sarah's ears! It was so good to be back in Italy. She'd spoken fluent Italian when she'd been younger and she was relieved to find her command of the language was coming back. She could understand the phone conversation going on between Carlos and Signor Mendicci. They seemed to be firm friends.

Carlos was now giving his phone to the ground stewardess. She listened for a few moments to what Judy's father was saying before agreeing to his suggestion that Judy be allowed to go with Dottore Fellini.

'*Sì, sì, signor, no problema, non importa…*'

The ground hostess smiled as she handed over her responsibility for Judy to the two doctors as Signor Mendicci had requested.

With Carlos in charge now, they made for the taxi rank. Glancing sideways as Carlos helped her and Judy into a waiting taxi, she thought how her dear friend hadn't changed much over the years. She'd never really considered him in terms of whether he was good-looking or not before. He was simply Carlos, her surrogate big brother, her lifelong friend. But today she couldn't help noticing that he was looking particularly handsome in his executive suit. The classic Italian, tall, powerful, good-looking and very much the successful medical consultant.

How old was he now? Nine years older than she was, so he must be thirty-eight. But he still looked young and boyish. Funny, she'd thought him so grown up when she'd been five. He'd seemed grown up all her life but today he looked as if he was reversing the process and getting younger. Perhaps that was because she was getting older.

She smiled to herself as the taxi sped away from the airport. These nice thoughts she was having about Carlos were simply gratitude towards him for once again solving a problem for her. When you'd grown up with someone you couldn't consider them as anything but a dear friend.

She turned to look at the young girl sitting between herself and Carlos. 'Are you OK, Judy?'

Judy nodded. 'You won't leave me, will you, Sarah?'

'Not until I've handed you over to your father, Judy. How long is it since you were in Rome?'

'I think I was a baby. I don't remember.'

They were now driving along the Grande Raccordo Annulare, the ring road around Rome. Sarah found herself gripping the edge of her seat as the traffic thickened and agitated, impatient drivers sounded their horns.

Carlos leaned across. 'You look nervous, Sarah. You've forgotten what Italian drivers are like, haven't you?'

Sarah grinned. 'I thought London was bad enough, but Rome…!'

Carlos raised his hands in a typically Italian way. 'Don't worry! *Il conducert*, the driver is a good man.'

Sarah liked the way that Carlos had always switched from Italian to English when he was talking to her. She'd learned lots of useful phrases from him as a child. And she loved his charmingly accented English. Another of his traits was his immense energy. He never seemed tired.

The driver turned off at one of the exits and progressed along a wide tree-lined street with a magnificent Renaissance church on the corner. Further along the street, smart, modern shops stood side by side with older, lovingly preserved buildings boasting exquisite architecture.

In spite of her nagging problem, Sarah could feel her excitement mounting now that she was back in her favourite city. She was going to be living and working here in Rome! For the moment she wasn't going to worry too much about where she might be in a year's time. She looked out of the window again, trying to lose herself in the sights and sounds of this beautiful city.

'We're nearly at the hospital,' Carlos said, as the taxi drove along the road beside the Tiber. '*Ecce!* There's the Ospedale Tevere!'

Sarah could see a large sign indicating the way to the hospital.

'Ospedale Tevere, the Tiber Hospital. What a lovely position, right beside the river.'

'We were very lucky to be able to build a brand-new hospital like this one. The site was donated by a rich benefactor who'd inherited the land. For years we've needed another hospital in this area. Other wealthy people, including Pietro Mendicci, donated money to help in the construction of the building. I was asked to organise the *Pronto Soccorso* department, which you call Accident and Emergency in England.'

'That must have been a challenge, starting up the department from scratch.'

Carlos smiled. 'Indeed it was. But it was also a great privilege to be able to implement the ideas I'd thought about while working in an older hospital. You'll be able to see for yourself whether my ideas work or not. I'm always open to further suggestions from my staff. Here we are!'

Carlos was already opening the car door.

'Are you hungry?' he asked as he helped Sarah out of the taxi.

'I am!' Judy said, jumping down onto the wide forecourt of the hospital.

Carlos smiled. 'We'll go to the medical staff canteen for lunch. What would you like, Judy?'

'Pizza, please.'

Carlos began to lead the way through the main entrance. '*Da questa parte, senora dottore, per favore*,' he said, holding back the door with an exaggerated flourish.

'What does that mean, Sarah?' Judy asked

'Carlos was simply saying, "This way, please, Doctor."'

Carlos raised his dark eyebrows. 'I thought Pietro Mendicci's daughter would speak Italian.'

'*Io non parlo italiano,*' Judy said, slowly and carefully. 'I don't speak Italian. That's the only phrase I know.'

'Oh, you will soon learn our language,' Carlos said in a jovial tone, as he escorted his guests into the crowded, noisy, medical canteen. 'Your papa will teach you,' he added, raising his voice above the general hubbub.

'If he has time,' Judy said quietly.

Sarah felt another pang of anxiety about the young girl. Coming out to an unknown situation by herself couldn't be easy. She sincerely hoped that Signor Mendicci, besides being a man who donated money to good causes, also believed that charity began at home.

Sarah and Carlos ate pasta linguini while Judy seemed to be enjoying her pizza. Looking around the room, Sarah decided that she could be in any medical canteen in Europe. There were carafes of house wine on the table which was the only thing that distinguished the place from her London hospital. The cream paintwork was also brighter and free from scuffs and scratches. Give it another five years of daily wear and tear!

The long, plastic-topped tables were close together and Sarah could hear snatches of earnest discussions about patients, amicable light-hearted chatter concerning a new opera, the latest stage play and a controversial article somebody had just read in the newspaper.

'I like the pizza, Sarah,' Judy said.

Sarah smiled, happy to see the improvement in Judy's condition. She hoped that Judy was going to live in a calm and tranquil environment here in Rome. It was obvious that the poor child had suffered a great deal from the situation in which she'd been forced to grow up. Putting down her fork as she finished her pasta, she saw a tall, distinguished-looking man coming into the large room. For a few seconds he looked around him before heading across towards their table.

'*Carlos, mi scusi per il disturbo...*'

'*Va benissimo. No problema, Pietro.*'

'I should have been at the airport to meet Judy,' Pietro Mendicci continued. 'But I had a business meeting and—'

'Please, Signor Mendicci, it has been a pleasure,' Carlos said, standing up and stretching out his hand. 'Your daughter is utterly charming.'

'Yes, she is! Pietro Mendicci embraced his daughter and started to say something in Italian to her.

'Sorry Dad, I can't speak Italian.'

'Don't worry, I will teach you. You will soon speak Italian now that you're coming to live with me permanently, my precious.'

Judy's eyes widened. 'I'm coming to live with you? But I thought I was just here for a holiday while Mummy and James were on honeymoon.'

Pietro looked embarrassed. 'Your mother didn't tell you? *Mi scusi!* Excuse me. I thought you knew that we had decided it would be better for everybody if you stayed with me.'

'Everybody? Nobody asked me.' A couple of tears escaped Judy's eyes and she bit her lip.

'I'm sorry, my precious. Your mother gave me the impression that—'

'It doesn't matter,' Judy said, wiping a hand across her face and smearing it with a streak of tomato sauce from the pizza.

Sarah reached across and gently removed the red mark with a tissue.

'I'd like to introduce my colleague, Dr Sarah Montgomery,' Carlos said.

'Judy had an asthmatic attack on the plane, Signor Mendicci.' Sarah said as they shook hands. 'It appears that the asthma, which was in remission, returned temporarily. I think Judy needs to be fully examined and assessed within the next few days so that her condition can be kept under control.'

'Would you be able to do that here at the hospital?'

'I'll make an appointment for Judy to be seen by a chest consultant as soon as possible,' Carlos said. 'Meanwhile if you're worried, Signor Mendicci, you must bring Judy in earlier.'

'Thank you. You have both been so kind.'

Carlos's pager was bleeping. He excused himself to go

over to the phone. Sarah glanced across and saw that he was frowning as he listened.

Judy gave Sarah a big hug and clung to her. 'I'm coming back to see you soon,' she said, as she took her father's outstretched hand.

'I shall look forward to seeing you again, Judy, and…'

Carlos returned to the table. 'Sarah, I have to go back to Pronto Soccorso. There's been a traffic pile-up on the Raccordo and some of the injured are being brought here.'

'*A presto*, see you soon. *Ciao!*' Pietro said as he took his daughter away.

'I'd like to come and help you,' Sarah said, falling into step with Carlos as he hurried towards the door.

'You would be extremely useful. Not too tired after your journey?'

'Of course not!'

The early morning queasiness had completely disappeared and while she was working she wasn't going to give another thought to the tiny life inside her. She was fully focussed on the job she'd been trained for.

Later, she would have time to take Carlos on one side and give him her news. But for a while they would both be too busy.

CHAPTER TWO

'DOTTORE! Per favore!'

Sarah was pulling on the white coat that Carlos had given her as she hurried into the large assessment area of the Pronto Soccorso, A and E department. Stretchers and trolleys carrying patients were arriving as quickly as the first batch of patients was being dealt with. The department was well staffed, but in typical Italian style the noise level seemed decidedly excessive to Sarah. At first, because of the background noise, she found it difficult to speak and think in Italian again, but quickly she forced herself to adjust to her new working conditions.

During the long summer holidays spent on the coast at the Villa Florissa as a child, she'd become fluent in Italian. Her command of Italian was, of necessity, quickly returning. She was totally immersed in the language.

She looked down at the young man on the trolley in front of her as she carefully removed the white dressing sheets covering his legs. The burns on his legs were red and wet so she assessed them as second degree. The patient's eyes were closed and from the low moaning sounds he was emitting it was obvious he was in considerable pain.

Plastic surgery would be needed at a later date when extensive treatment had been given over a period of time. Each burns case was different and the healing process could be long and slow. The main concern at the moment was to improve her patient's general condition and ensure that he didn't slip further into a state of shock.

Sarah glanced at the patient's admission notes. 'Giacomo, can you hear me?' she asked in Italian. No re-

22

sponse… 'Giacomo, I'm Dr Montgomery. If you can hear me—'

'We've sedated him, Doctor,' the paramedic said. 'He was in terrible pain when we managed to pull him out of the truck. His legs were on fire as we lifted him out. Only just made it before the whole thing blew up. Another minute and—'

'My legs!' the patient screamed, and began to swear.

Sarah's Italian was fully back by now, especially the colloquial bits. The poor man must be in agony. She squeezed his hand as she glanced at the medication chart the paramedic was holding. Another shot of morphine would help blur the edges.

Swiftly she injected her patient with the required dose before putting in a line so that she could administer some much-needed fluids intravenously. During severe burns cases like this, a large amount of the patient's circulating plasma could be lost. According to the details given at the scene of the accident, her patient was called Giacomo Lungara, aged twenty-eight.

She talked to Giacomo, hoping for some reply as she fixed up the bag of dextran and checked it was flowing freely.

He opened his eyes and stared up at Sarah as the fluid dripped steadily into his arm. *'Grazie, dottore.'*

Relief flooded through her as she heard Giacomo speak. 'How are you feeling now?'

The young man gave a wan smile. 'I'm still alive. You're English, aren't you, Doctor?'

She smiled. 'My accent gave me away, didn't it?'

'No, it was your beautiful smile. *Bellissima!*'

Despite his situation, Giacomo raised one hand to his lips and kissed it in a gallant, typically Italian gesture.

Perhaps her patient was in better general health than she'd feared when she'd first assessed him!

'Giacomo…'

'Call me Jack.' The patient switched to heavily accented English. 'I lived in your country for some years and everybody called me Jack… Ooh…'

Giacomo was grimacing and groaning again. 'Are my legs badly burned, Doctor? They feel… Aagh.'

'Your legs are going to need specialist treatment. It's essential you're cared for in a specialist burns unit, not here where there is a risk of infection from the other patients. I'm going to have you transferred as soon as possible,' Sarah said gently.

Her patient clung tightly to her hand. 'Are you coming with me?'

She glanced at Carlos who was attending to a patient on the next trolley.

'You can accompany Giacomo but please return as soon as possible, Sarah.' He signalled for a nurse and a porter to come across.

Giacomo continued to hold her hand as he was wheeled along the corridor to the burns unit. 'Sarah, what a pretty name. Sarah, Sarah…'

Sarah could tell that the medication she'd administered was having an effect on her patient. The pain had eased and Giacomo was becoming light-headed.

Her first impression of the layout of the Pronto Soccorso department was that it was extremely efficient. It appeared that there were several specialist units in close proximity to the main assessment and treatment areas where patients could be taken initially before they were transferred to the larger wards.

Giacomo was calmer when Sarah settled him in the small burns unit. As Mario Pellegrino, the plastic surgeon in charge, began to make his preliminary examination, Sarah explained that she had to return to Pronto Soccorso.

Mario nodded solemnly as he swabbed a badly burned area of thigh with sterile water.

'*Grazie, dottore,*' he murmured.

'*Prego.*'

Giacomo opened his eyes. 'You'll come back to see me, won't you Sarah?'

Sarah smiled. 'Of course I will.'

Back in A and E Carlos asked her to take over from him with the patient he was attending to.

'Rosa Clemente, age thirty,' he whispered, drawing Sarah to one side. 'The head injury is serious. The X-rays show there is a subdural haematoma. Please, continue to comfort her husband. He's very distraught. I have to relieve the pressure on the brain as soon as possible. There's a free theatre now so I'll go and scrub up.'

Sarah did what she could to console Rosa's husband but it was obvious that he'd come to realise the seriousness of his wife's condition.

'I don't know what I'll do without her,' he murmured. 'The children are at school. They don't know their mother is…'

The young father leaned forward in his chair, covering his face with his hands.

'Dr Fellini is an excellent surgeon,' Sarah said quietly. 'He will do all he can to save your wife.'

The man raised his tear-stained face towards Sarah. 'But if he can't save my Rosa… We were so happy together…so happy… Why did it have to be us?'

The man's poignant words remained with her throughout the rest of the day as she worked on her other patients. News from the scene of the multiple pile-up was filtering through in snatches of conversation among the paramedics and the patients' relatives. Apparently, the cause of the crash had been a series of events that had started with a dog running across the road. A little boy had run after the dog, causing the driver of a car transporter to swerve to avoid him.

The transporter had overturned and caused mayhem. It appeared that the dog had reached the other side of the road unharmed and the boy had mercifully escaped with cuts and bruises. Numerous cars were completely wrecked or burned out and three people had died at the scene of the crash. The driver of the transporter had still been breathing when he'd been loaded into the ambulance.

On examination, Sarah found the driver had multiple fractures and extensive internal injuries, and his breathing was drastically impaired due to the smoke he'd inhaled as his truck had burned. Sarah worked as part of a dedicated and experienced team but it was impossible to save his life. Along with two of her fellow doctors, the decision was taken that there was nothing more they could do. There were no longer any signs of life.

The most senior doctor switched off the respirator and wiped a tissue across his eyes before crossing the assessment area to take care of the next patient who was in need of his attention.

Sarah's lip was trembling as she pulled a sheet over her patient's face and signalled to one of the porters. She looked at the two nurses and one of the doctors who'd been helping her in the struggle to keep their patient alive. The younger of the two nurses had tears in her eyes. Sarah swallowed hard. This was possibly the first death the girl had witnessed. Maria would never forget this harrowing experience just as she herself couldn't forget her first experience of losing a patient, the old lady in the cancer ward who'd held onto Sarah's hand until she'd simply slipped away.

'We did all we could, Maria,'

'I know but—'

'Both of you nurses, go and take a few minutes' break. Have a strong cup of coffee,' Sarah said quietly. 'I'll finish off here.'

As the afternoon wore on, Sarah was aware that Carlos in Theatre was dealing with extremely difficult life-or-death cases. She had transferred a couple of patients for immediate surgery to him. Some of her patients were well enough to leave the hospital after their treatment, but many more had to be admitted.

She was relieved when Carlos, still in theatre greens, arrived back in the department, seemingly unaffected by his demanding workload.

'How is Rosa Clemente, the subdural haematoma?' she asked anxiously.

'As far as I can tell at this stage, the operation was a success. Our consultant neurologist is assessing the situation.'

Sarah smiled. 'Rosa's husband will be so relieved.'

Carlos nodded. 'Yes, he's with her now in Intensive Care. The next few hours will be critical but we've got a good team looking after her. Because we were able to relieve the pressure on the brain early on, I'm fairly confident that Rosa will pull through.'

'That's good news.'

Carlos narrowed his eyes as he looked at Sarah. 'It's time you stopped working. Theoretically, you shouldn't have been on duty today,' he said, peeling off his surgical gloves and tossing them into the bin. 'Thanks for all your help. The emergency situation is well under control now. I'll ask one of the nurses to take you to your room in the residents' quarters.'

'*Grazie, Carlos.*'

He put out his hand and touched her arm. 'And then, if you're not too tired, perhaps after you've showered and changed you might like to have supper with me. Not in the staff canteen, I hasten to add.'

Sarah smiled. She'd been worried that she wasn't going to see any more of Carlos today.

'I'd like that very much.'

'We haven't had time to catch up on each other's news. Have you anything exciting to report from England?'

She hesitated. She hadn't given a thought to her personal predicament during the course of the long afternoon.

'Not much to report actually, but—'

'Well, you can tell me all about the fascinating scene in London. I'm sure you lead a full social life, going to the theatre, seeing the latest films.'

'Oh, my life is one continual whirl of amusement.'

Her sarcasm seemed lost on Carlos.

He gave her a curt nod before moving away to deal with another patient.

'Well, then, I look forward to our evening, Sarah.'

As Carlos waited in the foyer of the residents' quarters he couldn't think why he was feeling so nervous. It was only Sarah he was taking out. His surrogate little sister who'd come running to him when she'd fallen off the garden swing and insisted he put a bandage on her knee so that she could play hospitals!

He sat down on one of the chairs near the revolving door and looked out across the busy road towards the river. The lights were slanting across the Tiber. Well-lit boats were gliding slowly past. He hoped Sarah would approve of the restaurant he was taking her to. He'd no idea how sophisticated her tastes were nowadays.

In his mind's eye he could still remember the first time he'd taken Sarah and her twin sister Lucy to a *gelateria* and bought both of them dishes of tutti-frutti ice cream. Half of Sarah's ice cream had ended up down the front of her blouse and her mother hadn't been too pleased. Lucy had managed to stay clean.

Strange that although the twins were identical they were so different in character. Sarah was the quick, impulsive, carefree one. Lucy appeared more serious, cautiously taking her time to assess each situation and never rushing into things. But it was Sarah who'd captured his heart with her winning ways.

He smiled to himself as he thought how he'd wished she really had been his little sister. But tonight he was distinctly nervous because the grown-up Sarah was different to the little girl he'd doted on. He hadn't seen her for a couple of years but they'd conversed over the phone and exchanged e-mails.

Perhaps it was working with her today that had finally forced him to make the transition from big brother to friend. They were on an equal footing now. She was no longer the child who'd looked up to him as the source of all grown-up knowledge.

He wondered, fleetingly, if he'd deliberately made the effort to think of her as a little girl. Perhaps he hadn't wanted her to grow up. Perhaps he'd known that if he'd acknowledged she was a real woman he would have to adjust his manner towards her. And accept the fact that she was devastatingly attractive and that he couldn't help feeling…well…he'd experienced disturbing vibes when he met her at the airport today. There was no doubt in his mind now that she was all woman and—

'Ah, there you are, Sarah.'

He watched as she walked confidently across the tiled floor towards him. A warm black winter coat enveloped her slender figure. Her blonde hair shone as if she'd just washed it. But it was the dazzling smile that intrigued him most. He'd never noticed her luscious, enticing lips before. She wore minimum make-up, which he approved of. Sarah

didn't need make-up. She was beautiful enough without it.
Bellissima!

'So where are we going, Carlos?'

Carlos put an arm in the small of Sarah's back as he
guided her towards the main door.

'To a secret location. I'm glad you're on time because
I've got a taxi waiting outside.'

As they left the foyer together, Sarah couldn't resist a
backward glance at the receptionist in charge of the desk.
A couple of nurses were also standing by, watching Carlos
and herself leave for an evening out. She felt proud to be
going out for the evening with the distinguished-looking,
handsome *specialista del Pronto Soccorso*.

As she climbed into the yellow taxi she told herself to
keep a cool head! Carlos might look divine in his superbly
cut, thigh-hugging grey suit but essentially he was still only
Carlos. He hadn't changed at all over the years. On duty
today he'd been super-efficient, abrupt with her at times,
but she'd understood exactly where he was coming from.
That was one thing that was good about their relationship.
They understood each other completely. In spite of the age
gap she knew that Carlos was the best friend she'd ever
had.

Looking out through the taxi window, she told Carlos
that she was amazed how beautiful the river looked at night.

Carlos smiled and drew closer to her on the back seat.
He could smell her perfume and it was having a profoundly
unexpected effect on his senses! He was trying desperately
to remember that the desirable woman beside him was little
Sarah.

'I think all city rivers look better in the dark,' he said.
'Lights twinkling on the water, boats moving sedately past
each other, not hurrying because the night is young and…
It's the same in Paris.'

'I've only been to Paris once.'

'That's a terrible shame. I must take you there some time when—' He broke off, seemingly embarrassed. 'I mean, it's a big gap in your education, Sarah. But I'll be able to show you Rome while you're here.'

'I want to see all my favourite places again. The Colosseum, the Spanish Steps, the Roman Forum, everywhere! It's going to be so wonderful living here and…!'

She stopped speaking. 'What's the matter, Carlos? Why are you looking at me like that?'

'Like what?'

'Well, as if you had never seen me before.'

'Perhaps I haven't,' he said softly, as he deliberately moved away to the other side of the taxi. 'Just now when you were getting excited about Rome I thought I glimpsed the child in you. The Sarah I first knew. But you've changed.'

'I should hope so! You wouldn't want me to spill food down my blouse tonight, would you?'

Carlos laughed, and the palpable tension between them was broken. 'Funnily enough, I was thinking about that just before you arrived tonight. No, I certainly need you to act your age tonight.'

He turned and looked out of the window at a passing limousine. The way he was now feeling, he definitely wanted Sarah to be grown up! But how did she feel about him? He took a deep breath. This was a difficult situation, both of them adjusting to their new roles. He wasn't sure what his role with Sarah was any more. Wasn't sure how he was going to handle his increasingly changing ideas about her.

The taxi pulled up in front of the restaurant. He reached for his wallet.

'*Quanto è?* How much is it?'

Outside on the pavement, Sarah smiled at Carlos as the cab pulled away from the kerb.

'This looks nice. Rather posh and expensive, I would say.'

'I think you'll approve when we get inside. And if you're very good I'll buy you a tutti-frutti for dessert.'

'Fantastic!' Sarah entered into the spirit of the game, pretending their nostalgic world still existed.

Carlos put his hand under Sarah's elbow and guided her in through the revolving doors.

'A tutti-frutti with nuts?' she asked, her eyes twinkling.

Carlos laughed. 'The full works! Now, if you'd like to leave your coat in the cloakroom we'll meet in the bar. What shall I order for you?'

She grinned. 'Oh, it's got to be a Campari, hasn't it? When in Rome…'

'Wasn't that the first alcohol you ever tasted? The day you and Lucy decided you liked the pink colour of the bottle and decided to taste it.'

Sarah gave a wry grin. 'Lucy said it tasted like poison, but in the interests of science I nipped my nose and drank a large mouthful.'

'And promptly threw up on the carpet as I recall,' Carlos said dryly.

Sarah groaned. 'I thought I'd never ever drink Campari again, but I changed my mind as I got older.'

Carlos watched as Sarah disappeared into the cloakroom, pulling off her coat as she went. Underneath she was wearing a stunning little black dress. Her skirt had ridden up as she'd been sitting in the car and she was displaying a generous amount of slender legs that looked as if they went up to her armpits.

He hurried to the bar and ordered a couple of Camparis, drinking deeply from his own as soon as it was placed in front of him. He needed that!

In the cloakroom, Sarah removed her coat and smoothed down her dress, glancing in the mirror to check her appearance. She was paler than usual. When she'd come off duty she'd felt decidedly queasy again. The hormonal changes in her body during the first weeks of pregnancy were upsetting her usually robust constitution. Whilst she'd been battling to save lives in Pronto Soccorso she hadn't had time to think about herself.

She'd deliberately ignored all thoughts about her pregnancy as she'd showered and changed. This was one problem that would have to be put on hold. But for how long? Her predicament wasn't going to go away. The baby was growing all the time. Still very small at the moment but systematically taking what it needed from her body to build itself into a healthy, living…

Oh, heavens! She clamped her hands over her mouth to stop herself from shrieking out. She'd forgotten about the baby when she'd ordered a Campari. She didn't want her baby to taste strong spirits at this delicate stage of its development. Only ten per cent of the alcohol filtered through to the baby so a glass of wine or champagne wouldn't harm it, but spirits were definitely out.

'*Tutto bene, signorina?*' asked the kindly woman who'd taken her coat. 'Is everything all right?'

'*Molto bene, grazie,*' Sarah said, forcing herself to smile. 'I'm fine.'

As she walked along the ornate high-ceilinged corridor that led to the bar she realised with excitement that for the first time she was one hundred per cent sure that she wanted to go ahead with the pregnancy. There was no question that she wouldn't have a termination now.

But there were still so many problems ahead of her to be faced! The reality of being a single mum was daunting, to say the least. Working in A and E during her pregnancy, deciding where to have the baby, where to live, childcare after the birth when she returned to work…not to mention coping with Robin's reaction to the news!

She took a deep breath. She mustn't spoil her first evening with Carlos by being worried and trying to offload her problems on him. For this evening she would try to pretend that she hadn't a care in the world.

She moved her lips and attempted a broad, happy smile as Carlos came towards her.

'What are you smiling about?' Carlos said as he left the bar and guided Sarah to a small table.

A waiter followed them, carrying two glasses of Campari.

'I was thinking how nice it is to relax after my long day,' Sarah said quickly, as she sat down on the chair that Carlos was holding out for her.

She turned to the waiter and asked if he would bring her a glass of freshly squeezed orange juice.

'I've changed my mind about the Campari, Carlos. Too much alcohol will make me sleepy.'

'Nothing wrong with that,' Carlos said huskily. 'It's good to relax completely in the evening.'

'Yes, but my day started a long time ago in darkest London. I feel as if I've been awake for days.'

Carlos nodded. 'I'm sure you do. Don't worry, I've scheduled you to start late tomorrow so you can have... What do you English call it when you stay in bed?'

Sarah smiled. 'A lie-in. That would be lovely. Thanks.'

And if she felt as queasy, as she had done this morning, she would have time to pull herself together before she went on duty. Carlos was being very considerate with her.

She hesitated. It might be an idea to broach the subject of her pregnancy tonight while Carlos was in a relaxed mood. If she was positive in her approach and didn't admit how worried she really was, it wouldn't spoil their evening, would it? She'd much rather speak to him as a friend than go to see him in his consulting room at the hospital.

She took a deep breath as she turned towards him. But

Carlos was speaking to the waiter who'd brought her orange juice.

'Would you like to see the menu?'

'Si, signor.' The waiter hurried away.

'Carlos…'

'We can look at the menus while we have our drinks, Sarah. Cheers!'

They clinked glasses. Sarah sipped her deliciously cold drink and placed the glass back on the table. The moment had gone. She'd plucked up her courage, but now the doubts about her future were flooding back. All these wretched hormones swirling around her body!

But all she had to do was tell Carlos that—

'So how are your parents?'

Sarah recognised that the right moment had passed. She'd better try to forget her pregnancy and be as normally sociable as she could.

'Mum's busy as ever with her committee work. She's chairman of the parish council and secretary of the village social committee. Dad potters about in the garden and does the crossword. He's not fully recovered from his stroke but he does as much as he can. He worked so hard when he was company chairman that I think he simply enjoys the fact that he has absolutely no pressures on his time nowadays.'

Yes, postponing her discussion on pregnancy and talking about her family was helping her to feel normal again.

'And are they still in that great big house in Yorkshire?'

'Yes, they are. Lucy and I are always suggesting they should move into something smaller but Mum insists she's happy where she is. And Dad always goes along with Mum.'

Carlos grinned. 'Everyone agrees with your mum. I used to be terrified of her when I was younger. That was the reason I agreed to babysit for you and Lucy in the first place.'

Sarah looked surprised. 'You mean my mother talked you into looking after us?'

Carlos nodded. 'It started one day when I was sixteen. Your father was in England, I remember. You and Lucy must have been about seven. The babysitter cancelled at the last minute and your mother was furious. She had tickets for a concert, I remember. She came round to our house, said you two were in bed and could I possibly sit in and listen to check that you were OK from time to time. My mother said there was no reason why I couldn't take my homework round and work at your house. I can remember I didn't feel too pleased about the idea, but your mother made me an offer I couldn't refuse.'

'You mean, Mum paid you to look after us!'

'On this occasion she did. When I got to know you I didn't mind keeping an eye on you occasionally.'

Sarah smiled. 'I remember we didn't want the usual babysitter to come back. She wasn't as much fun as you were.'

'Your mother tried to talk you into having her back but you both insisted you didn't like her any more. Which was difficult for your mother, because she was on her own in the Villa Florissa for most of the summer, wasn't she?'

Sarah nodded. 'Dad took his job very seriously. He could only spare two or three weeks for a holiday with us, so Mum made her own life out there. Typical Mum, she had a busy social life so a babysitter was essential.'

'Your mother certainly got involved in everything. She was tireless in her charity work so everybody wanted her on their committees. Taking along a couple of small energetic girls to meetings just wasn't an option.'

Sarah frowned. 'So all those times when you took us out

for ice cream or down to the beach, did you have to be talked into it?'

'No! I soon found I enjoyed being with you as if you were my little sisters. I'd always hated being an only child of older parents and it was like being part of a young family. And the pair of you were always so incredibly lively that we had some great times together.'

Sarah reached across the table and squeezed Carlos's hand. 'I'm glad you said that. I wouldn't want to think Lucy and I had just been a chore. I've got such happy memories of being with you as a child.'

She let her hand rest on his for a few seconds, surprised at the tingling feeling of excitement that was flooding through her. It was good to be here in this restaurant with dear Carlos. Raising her eyes to his, she saw that he was looking at her in a decidedly quizzical manner. His mouth was set in a severe line as if he was displeased about something. Perhaps he hadn't wanted to tell her the babysitter story.

Carlos watched as Sarah removed her hand and began to study the menu. He could feel that he was breathing more rapidly. Why had Sarah squeezed his hand like that? Just when he'd been reminding himself that he wanted to think of her as his younger sister he'd felt his body coming alive at the touch of her slender fingers. If he found himself disturbed by a casual squeeze of the hand, he'd better be careful when he kissed her goodnight to make sure his lips didn't stray from her cheeks!

He looked down at the menu the waiter had given him and tried hard to concentrate. Sarah had lifted her head and was smiling across the table at him.

'Fresh artichokes—my favourite!' Sarah exclaimed enthusiastically. 'I'd like to start with that, followed by the *scaloppine al marsala*. I love those small escalopes in Marsala sauce.'

'Don't you want some pasta to start with?'

Carlos realised he must try to restore the emotional balance by playing the older platonic friend.

Sarah smiled impishly and Carlos thought how beautiful she looked now that she'd reached a certain stage of beguiling maturity. He'd thought she was pretty as a child. But now, with the added impetus of his growing feelings for her, he found it difficult to remain impartial. Did everyone in the room think he was a lucky man to have such an attractive woman with him?

'I know it's traditional to have an antipasta,' Sarah began slowly, as if she didn't want Carlos to be displeased with her. 'But I would be too full to eat my main course.'

'Perhaps a little minestrone soup for the signorina?' the waiter, hovering nearby, suggested.

Sarah agreed to have some soup, mentally noting that it would be good for the baby.

They were shown to a table in a corner of the restaurant. The window overlooked a busy piazza, where Sarah could see people sitting outside the bars and restaurants, their coats pulled snugly round them as they drank their coffee or sipped glasses of wine. It was only January, but apart from the profusion of winter coats and jackets it could have been a balmy summer evening.

Couples were strolling around the square hand in hand, oblivious to the fact that it was a winter evening. Sarah thought about the freezing cold London she'd left behind and felt glad she'd made the move. But making the transition from single woman to single mum would have been much easier if she'd stayed in England. There were going to be far more problems if she continued working in Rome with a baby.

Once again she told herself to stop worrying. She had to make the most of her evening with Carlos, the first for a long time. She couldn't remember when she'd last had him all to herself like this.

'Do your parents still have an apartment in Rome?' she asked quickly.

Carlos nodded. 'They live in Rome all the year now. They rent out the two houses they own on the coast.'

'You mean the one you used to live in and the Villa Florissa, the one our family rented for the summer holidays, don't you? Do you ever go down there?'

'My parents sometimes ask me to go and check that everything's OK. The tenants usually have a list of repairs or alterations they'd like me to sort out so I have to get onto the local workmen. Occasionally it takes a few days before I get everything sorted.'

'Ah, I'd love to see the house where we used to stay,' Sarah said, picking up her soup spoon.

'Would you? Perhaps I can arrange it some time.'

Carlos turned away to look out of the window. What was that saying about never going back? Maybe it would be a mistake to become too nostalgic with Sarah. But she seemed keen to return to the Villa Florissa. She must have happy memories.

'It's difficult, arranging the off-duty schedule,' he said quietly, 'but I'll see what I can do to make sure we get some time off together.'

'I'd like that.'

'Would you?'

For a moment their eyes met over the table. Sarah felt a warm glow of happiness stealing over her. Yes, once she'd confided in Carlos she would feel better. He was such a dear friend. So kind, so... What was she waiting for? She could hear Carlos talking about the off-duty schedule now. She ought to stop daydreaming about the baby and concentrate.

'The trouble with being in charge of organising the off-duty schedule is that everybody thinks I can work it around their own special needs. I'm as accommodating as I can be but sometimes I simply have to be firm.'

'It must be difficult for you.'

'Yes, it is at times. But, then, there are some members of staff who never ask for any favours regarding duty, even when they're going through a difficult time. Take Helena, for example. She's one of the senior doctors in my department. We worked together at my last hospital and I gave her a good reference when she asked for a transfer to Ospedale Tevere. Even when she became pregnant she didn't ask for any preferential treatment.'

'Was she able to work through her pregnancy?'

'Until the last few weeks. I made sure she had time off for her antenatal examinations and I tried to ease her workload wherever I could. She works two days a week now because it's not easy to work full time with a baby.'

Sarah kept her eyes firmly fixed on her plate as she toyed with an artichoke. There was nothing wrong with this particular artichoke except it suddenly seemed as if it had assumed the consistency of cardboard. She put down her fork as Carlos's words hit home. No, it wouldn't be easy to work full time with a baby, but she herself would need a full-time salary! Two days a week wouldn't pay the bills for a flat, childcare, food, clothes…

She lifted her head and looked across the table. 'So, presumably, Helena has a husband who is financially OK?'

Carlos shook his head. 'Helena's a single mum. She doesn't have a husband. She had a boyfriend who left her when she told him she was pregnant. But she has a small legacy from her grandmother, I believe. She copes extremely well on her own.'

'She sounds interesting.'

'Yes. I wish all the staff were as easy to manage. I'd like to hand over the job of duty rosters to Administration but they won't take on the responsibility. Apparently, because I'm in charge of the department I understand the needs of my staff better than they do.'

Sarah folded and refolded the starched white napkin on her lap as she looked across the table. Yes, she was sure that Carlos did understand the needs of his staff. Was this the time to tell him of her own needs?

She swallowed hard. No. She was feeling very emotional and if she started talking about all the problems this pregnancy was posing she might begin to cry. And that would be highly embarrassing in this posh restaurant! Besides, she had to come to terms with the situation in her own way. Make her own decisions about what she was going to do. She couldn't simply offload her problems on Carlos.

He was her dear friend but he was also her boss. When she had to ask for time off to go for her antenatal examinations or to go looking for somewhere to live or any one of the unknown situations she had yet to face…

'I thought you liked artichokes, Sarah!'

'I do…I'm just not very hungry.'

'Well, how about some dessert?'

Sarah shook her head, but agreed to a coffee. After the first sip she knew it had been a mistake to have ordered it. Espresso coffee had been her favourite, especially in Italy, but tonight, for the first time in her life, it tasted bitter and unpleasant. It was a well-known fact that pregnant women often went off tea and coffee. The queasiness was returning. She could feel her head going light again. She wasn't going to faint, was she?

She gripped the side of the table, hoping the dizzy spell would pass off.

'Sarah, are you OK?'

Carlos was leaning over her, his arm around her shoulder. She looked up into his concerned brown eyes.

'I'm tired that's all. It's been a long day.'

'Of course! You must be exhausted. I'll get the bill and take you back to the hospital.'

In the taxi, Carlos put an arm loosely but protectively round her shoulders.

'Sarah, are you OK?'

'I'm fine!' Her stock answer even when she felt exhausted. She closed her eyes and leaned against Carlos. The feel of his rock-solid muscular frame was very comforting.

'I hope I'm not spoiling your evening by being a party-pooper,' she said quietly.

'A party what?'

'It's a silly expression meaning to leave the party early.'

'No, no, of course not.' Carlos squeezed her shoulders in what he hoped would be taken as a friendly gesture. That was all it was meant to be…wasn't it?

He held his breath as a frisson of something akin to desire surged through him. Here he was in the back of a cab with the most gorgeous blonde and he was desperately trying to dampen down his feelings for her. What a waste of a romantic situation! But, then, what did you do when a child from the past grew up and turned out to be something infinitely more than you'd ever wanted her to be? Why couldn't Sarah have grown up to be plain and undesirable?

But a little voice inside him said that he was actually enjoying the new-found attraction he was feeling for Sarah. If only she felt the same way about him, what would be the harm in taking their relationship a step further?

If Sarah felt the same way! That was the criterion. And until she gave him a definite sign that his feelings were reciprocated he wasn't going to chance making a move. Their friendship was too fragile. He couldn't afford to lose her altogether, not now when he'd found out just how precious she was to him.

The taxi was pulling into the hospital forecourt. Carlos

got out and paid the driver before helping Sarah to alight. She really did look exhausted, poor girl. He'd better get her back to her room in the residents' quarters as soon as possible. And no stopping off at his room for a drink! Another time soon, he hoped, when Sarah wasn't so tired.

Sarah linked her arm through Carlos's as they walked along the corridor towards her room. Rows of anonymous doors on either side. She wondered, fleetingly, which door belonged to Carlos. He was probably housed in a much more exalted section of the building than these basic rooms. She toyed with the idea of asking him in for coffee but the thought of working out how the cafetière machine worked defeated her in her weary state. Apart from that, she'd gone off coffee.

They stood outside her door, Sarah searching the depths of her bag for the key.

'I won't ask you in. I haven't finished unpacking and everything's in a mess. Thank you so much for a lovely evening, Carlos.'

She turned towards him and reached up to kiss him good-night on his cheek. That was what she meant to do at the beginning, but either she'd become intoxicated by his sexy, evocative aftershave or she'd simply succumbed to the longing to get closer to him, but somehow their lips met in the middle. She knew she'd instigated this, she knew it was her place to pull away. This wasn't a simple friendly kiss she was savouring. Carlos seemed to be enjoying it too...

Sarah closed her eyes and gave herself up to the excitement running through her. She wanted to make the most of this deliciously wicked moment. It was only a moment, but it was an exquisitely sensual experience...

What on earth was she doing, standing here, feeling limp and excited, hoping the night was just beginning? She'd been dog tired but not any more!

Carlos reached his hand above her head, supporting himself against the doorpost as he looked down at her with a decidedly tender expression in his eyes.

'Goodnight, Sarah,' he said huskily. 'It's been wonderful to be with you again.'

And then he turned and walked quickly away. She watched until he reached the end of the corridor and disappeared from sight before she went inside her room. As soon as she'd closed the door she leaned against it, taking deep breaths to calm herself.

Wow! That had been some kiss! She'd never thought of Carlos as a sex symbol before but, heavens above, her knees were trembling with excitement! It was a good thing he had gone otherwise she might have made a fool of herself. And she had no intention of doing that. Carlos was her dear sweet friend and…

But he was an infinitely desirable friend, she realised. If she could forget the fact that he'd been her babysitter, that he regarded her as his little sister, she could really fall for him in a big way!

A sudden flash of memory reminded her of the childish crush she'd had on Carlos when she'd been about nine. He'd just been accepted as a medical student and Sarah had decided that she wanted to be a doctor just like Carlos. She'd been excited when her mother had said he was going to babysit that evening while she went out to one of her meetings.

But he'd brought round his current girlfriend and it had been difficult to ignore the awful pangs of jealousy she'd felt when she'd heard them talking and laughing downstairs while she and Lucy had been in their bedroom.

She vividly remembered how she'd tiptoed downstairs and seen them sitting on the sofa, kissing! Carlos had looked up and told her to go back to bed. Oh, the shame of being dismissed in such a peremptory manner by her idol! When she'd confided in Lucy, her sister had said she was being stupid. Carlos was a grown-up now. He wouldn't look twice at a little kid like Sarah.

And she'd believed her. Until now. Now that she was really grown up, was there a chance that Carlos might be considering her in a different light?

She groaned aloud. Not now that she was pregnant. It wouldn't be fair to lead him on and try to show him that she was a desirable female. Her life was on hold until after the baby was born. Carlos wouldn't fancy her once he knew she was pregnant.

Pregnant with another man's child. How undesirable could she get?

CHAPTER THREE

AT THE end of the first week, Carlos called Sarah into his office. From the moment she stepped foot into his private space, she could see that Carlos was in professional mode. In fact, he'd been completely professional with her since their evening out together. When they'd been working together in hospital, surrounded by staff and patients, there had been no hint that the evening had meant anything to him other than an occasion when two old friends had caught up on each other's news.

As she lowered herself into the leather upholstered chair at the side of Carlos's large mahogany desk she felt decidedly nervous. This was the first time they'd been alone since that kiss. The kiss that had seemed so significant to her at the time but which had obviously meant nothing to Carlos.

'You wanted to see me, Carlos?'

Carlos fiddled with his silver pen as he looked across the desk. He'd been longing to talk to Sarah by herself, but he was unwilling to risk spoiling their friendship. He didn't know what to make of the way she'd clung to him that evening. The way she'd seemed to want to prolong that decidedly sexy embrace. He'd had to hold himself in check to make sure he hadn't carried her along to his room and torn her clothes off, caveman style!

From the vibes he'd been receiving and the sexy way Sarah had suddenly behaved that night, he'd felt she would have welcomed his advances. But just as he'd begun to luxuriate in the sensation of kissing her in a madly uncharacteristic way, a sane voice inside his head had been urging him to cool it. This was Sarah, his lifelong platonic friend, and he didn't want to lose her.

If he changed the mood of their relationship it could ruin everything. And another thing he must always remember was that they had to work together without embarrassment. So for the last week he'd simply pretended that the unexpectedly sexy, positively erotic kiss hadn't happened. Whenever he'd been working with Sarah, she'd seemed relieved that the kiss had been unimportant.

Carlos cleared his throat. 'We've both been too busy to talk to each other since…since we went out to the restaurant together. I wanted to tell you that you seem to be settling into the department extremely well. I've been amazed at the way you've immersed yourself in our language. Your Italian was fluent when you were younger but I hadn't expected you would cope so well initially.'

Sarah could feel herself beginning to relax. 'I've always enjoyed speaking Italian and I like reading Italian novels. A friend of mine on the hospital staff in London was Italian. She lent me some of her medical books and we used to spend time talking in Italian during our off duty while we were discussing medical terminology.'

'Well, it's certainly paid off.' Carlos hesitated before continuing. 'Several of our colleagues have told me they're impressed with your efficiency and…'

He put the pen down and leaned forward. 'Sarah, it's so difficult to be in charge of the department you're working in and remain detached. I hope that doesn't sound pretentious but I've got to write a report on my initial impression of your capabilities. You seem to have settled into the department extremely well. Do you have any problems you'd like to discuss with me?'

She took a deep breath. Now was the time when she should confess about the baby…no, she would leave it another week. Allow herself to really get the hang of the place before she dropped her bombshell.

After a great deal of thought, she'd decided that she was going to stay in Rome and sort out all the problems of being a single working mum. But occasionally, during the past week, she'd wondered if it wouldn't be better to take the easy way out and go back to England.

That was when her stubborn streak had taken over! She'd never been a quitter. Other women coped with single parenthood, and so would she. If she didn't frighten herself by looking too far ahead, she would get through.

It was early days. After all, lots of women didn't realise they were pregnant until they were two or three months. If she hadn't done that test she wouldn't have known. She was only seven weeks now so when she did announce her pregnancy it would be assumed that she'd only just found out.

'No problems, Carlos.'

Carlos nodded before glancing nervously down at his notes. He wasn't sure how to handle this next bit.

'There was just one complaint, Sarah…well, hardly a complaint, more of an observation. Sister Lucia said you'd kept her waiting one morning. You'd agreed to talk to some of the junior nurses about resuscitation techniques. She'd phoned your room to see if you were coming and you'd said you'd been unavoidably delayed but would be along in a few minutes.'

Carlos waited for Sarah to respond. She remained very still as she considered her answer.

'I wasn't feeling very well,' she began hesitantly.

What an understatement! When the phone had rung, she'd been chucking up in the loo, kneeling on the floor, hanging onto the basin while the room had spun around her.

'What was the problem?'

She crossed her fingers behind her back. 'I woke up with a bad headache so it took me longer than usual to get ready.'

'Perhaps you could have phoned the department?'

'I'm sorry, Carlos…'

She raised her eyes to his and saw that he was looking at her with an enigmatic expression on his handsome face. She knew she should have phoned the department, but she'd been feeling too ill.

Carlos stood up and came round the desk, leaning down to touch her face.

'Don't look so sad,' he said gently, all traces of his former professionalism having disappeared. 'You're doing an excellent job. I may be in charge but I'm also the man who has to listen to both sides of every story and keep everyone happy. You are happy here, aren't you, Sarah?'

She nodded, unable to speak for a few seconds. 'I like working here very much,' she said carefully. 'I—'

The phone rang. 'Excuse me,' Carlos said. 'Carlos Fellini…'

He listened, then replaced the receiver. 'I'm needed in A and E. Helena wants some help with a patient. Come with me, Sarah.'

As they hurried along the corridor together, Sarah asked Carlos if Helena was the doctor he'd told her about the other evening, the one who had a baby.

'Yes, today is one of the two days that Helena is working this week. I'm surprised you remember me talking about her. Why do you ask?'

Carlos held back the swing doors to allow a porter pushing a trolley to pass through on his way to X-Ray.

'No reason, Carlos. I just like to get to know my colleagues.'

'I'm glad you feel like that. It helps the smooth running of the department when colleagues understand each other.'

Maria was waiting for them. Sarah followed Carlos into the cubicle that the nurse indicated.

'Helena, this is Sarah, the doctor from England I told you about.'

The small, dark-haired woman shook hands with Sarah before giving them details concerning the patient who was lying on the examination couch. Apparently, forty-year-old Marcellina had collapsed at work. Helena was concerned that the preliminary tests she'd done were indicating the possibility that the kidneys weren't functioning properly.

'I've put everything in the notes here, Carlos. Would you mind taking over from me? I need some time off to go along to the crèche. I've just had a call from one of the nursery staff to say that Teresa has been sick. I'd like to check that—'

'Yes, of course you must go to your baby,' Carlos said, quickly. 'Let me know if you need to take the rest of the day off.'

'You are very understanding, Carlos.'

Carlos smiled. 'I like to help my staff when there is a family problem, Helena.'

Sarah moved quickly towards the door so that she could have a quick word with Helena before she left.

'Is it difficult to cope with work when you have a baby to care for, Helena?'

Helena, with her hand on the door, looked surprised by the question. 'I couldn't cope with full-time work any more. Two days a week is all I can manage now. But I do look forward to my days in hospital. It can be very lonely on your own with a baby. I intend to come back full time when Teresa is older. I asked Carlos if he could keep my job open for me and he promised to do what he could. He's so helpful, don't you think?'

Sarah nodded. 'Yes, he is. Nice to meet you, Helena. We must have another chat when we both have more time.'

Sarah hurried back to the examination cubicle where she listened as Carlos talked quietly to their patient. It appeared that Marcellina had been feeling ill for about a year.

Sarah leaned across and took hold of the patient's cold, clammy hand. 'In what way have you been feeling ill, Marcellina?'

The patient frowned as she shifted her head on the pillow. 'I'm always tired, and look at my hair! It's so thin now you can see the scalp, can't you?'

'What's your job?' Carlos asked.

'I'm a teacher. I teach physical education.' The patient gave a harsh laugh. 'Maybe I'm getting too old to run around now that I'm forty. I went to the doctor because my back was always aching. He gave me lots of painkillers but they didn't help much.'

'How long have you been taking painkillers?' Sarah asked.

'Oh, a year or two, maybe longer.'

Further questioning elicited that Marcellina often took a double dose to ease her pain.

'Have you any idea what might be wrong with me?'

'Not until we've done further tests. I'm going to admit you to our preliminary medical unit,' Carlos said.

The patient looked relieved. 'At last somebody's going to find out why I'm feeling like this! I've been worried for so long and nobody's taken me seriously. Can I call my husband to tell him where I am?'

'Your school secretary already did that,' Maria said, coming into the cubicle. 'Your husband is waiting to see you when the doctors have finished their examination.'

'So, what's your theory about Marcellina?' Carlos said, after their patient had been taken to the preliminary medical unit.

Sarah leaned against the edge of the examination couch.

'It's a complex case. The initial tests show possible damage to the kidneys. That was probably caused by her excessive use of painkillers.'

Carlos nodded. 'I'm sure it was. So, first we have to eliminate the painkillers, then treat the kidney problem.'

'After which we must find out why Marcellina was so tired in the first place.'

'Any theories on that one?' Carlos asked.

Sarah hesitated. 'I've a hunch it might be a thyroid imbalance.'

'Why?'

Sarah frowned reflectively. 'Marcellina must have been basically very fit when she trained to be a PE teacher. I had a similar patient only a few months ago. She'd been a dancer for several years but more recently had found she was always tired. Finally she collapsed under the strain of running a home and looking after her children. It turned out her problem was an underactive thyroid.'

Carlos leaned forward. 'You could be right. That's one of the tests I asked the laboratory to do. But we have to consider other diagnoses. Hepatitis C causes the same long-term lethargy, lack of energy and general ill health.'

Sarah nodded. 'Yes, we're checking on that as well, aren't we? I'd like to follow up this case, Carlos. It intrigues me.'

Carlos smiled approvingly. 'Of course, that's one of the reasons why we keep our patients in the preliminary units when they're first admitted, so that the doctors who admitted them can be involved in the subsequent treatment. Sometimes the first doctor who sees a patient can remember something that's crucial to the final diagnosis.'

'So where will Marcellina be cared for during the next few days?'

'Marcellina will be in the preliminary medical unit until we've established a firm diagnosis. The medical staff there will be pleased to have you liaise with them and follow up the case. Talking of which—following up a case, that is— the burns case you admitted was asking about you earlier this morning, saying he hadn't seen you for a couple of days.'

Sarah smiled. 'You mean Jack.'

'Jack? Unusual name for an Italian truck driver.'

'Giacomo asked me to call him Jack. He used to live in England.'

Carlos raised an eyebrow. 'Well, you've certainly made a good impression on him.'

'I'll go and see him for a few minutes when I've got time.'

'And Judy Mendicci, your young asthma patient, is seeing the chest consultant this morning. Her father phoned me to see if he could bring his daughter along to the department to see the kind lady doctor who helped her on the plane.'

'I'd love to see Judy,' Sarah said, as she and Carlos left the cubicle and went back into the main section of the department.

'*Per favore*, will you come over here, Dottore Montgomery?' Lucia called. 'I need help with this patient.'

'You take care of that patient, Sarah,' Carlos said quickly. 'Maria just asked me if I would help with a newly arrived suspected fractured pelvis. I've got to go to X-Ray so that I can liaise with the X-ray and orthopaedic staff.'

For the rest of the day, Sarah didn't have a moment to herself. Besides the routine cuts requiring sutures, bones that needed X-rays before she could have them set or admitted for manipulation, there was a fire in a nearby shop. Six customers suffered smoke inhalation problems before they could be evacuated. After treating them, Sarah admitted two of the patients and allowed the other four to go home.

At the end of the afternoon, she realised she hadn't had time for lunch. No wonder she was beginning to feel queasy again. She made a mental note to start eating regularly now that she was pregnant. It was no good advising patients how to take care of themselves if she neglected herself.

And she hadn't had time to see Giacomo in the burns unit. She would have to make time as soon as possible. Judy, the other patient who'd asked to see her, had already been into the department with her father. Sarah had managed to spend a few minutes with them in between caring for her patients so that she could catch up on their news.

The chest consultant had apparently given Judy a nebuliser and some medication to be taken in the event of a further attack of asthma. He'd asked her father to make sure that Judy enjoyed a calm and tranquil home life.

'So this is what we're aiming for,' Pietro Mendicci had told Sarah as he'd put his arm round his small daughter. 'A tranquil family life. I'm hoping to take Judy with me to our house on the coast this weekend.'

'I'm going to meet my little stepsister and stepbrothers and my stepmother,' Judy said quietly. 'I've never seen them before. Daddy's got a house right on the beach where he lives with his wife and family when he's not in Rome.'

Pietro smiled. 'Judy's looking forward to joining the family, aren't you, Judy?'

Judy nodded, before looking up appealingly at Sarah. 'Do you think they'll like me?'

'I'm sure they will, Judy!'

Sarah glanced across at Pietro. He seemed to have good intentions and, after all, according to Carlos he was a good-living, philanthropic man. As Pietro went away with his daughter, Sarah fervently hoped that Judy would fit in well with her new family and not become distressed again. The chest consultant was right. More than anything else Judy needed stability and a loving home. But all the money in the world couldn't buy love and happiness.

When Sarah finally found time to see Giacomo in the burns unit she told him she could only spend a few minutes with him.

'That's OK, Doctor,' Giacomo said, in English. 'You've cheered me up just by coming to visit me. I don't get many visitors.'

'I'm sorry about that.'

Sarah had put on a sterile gown as she'd come inside Giacomo's isolation room. The room was being kept at a constant temperature. Aseptic conditions were essential when burns were being treated by the exposure to air method. Complete with face mask, she leaned over to check on the burns injuries to his legs. She noted that coagulum was forming over the surface where the skin had been burned off. Once the surgeon had removed the coagulum it would be possible to do skin grafts.

After a few seconds she moved back and pulled her face mask down as she glanced at Jack's chart. Apparently, the antibiotic spray which had been used initially on the worst areas had been discontinued.

'Your injuries are looking much better, Jack.'

Jack pulled a wry face. 'My legs look weird to me. I mean, there's no skin left, is there? I can't walk around with that scabby stuff covering them, can I?'

'You'll be able to walk when you've had your skin grafts, Jack. The surgeon will first remove the coagulum— that's the scabby stuff you were talking about—and then he'll put small pieces of skin over the surface of your legs and then...'

'Where will they get the skin from, Sarah?'

'I've just been discussing your case with the consultant.

He's planning to take some skin from your bottom and some from the inside of your forearms…just here.'

Giacomo raised his arm and stared at the area that Sarah was indicating. 'Will it hurt?'

Sarah shook her head. 'You'll be given a general anaesthetic so you won't know anything at all about it.'

The patient put his arm down and raised himself on his elbows. 'Well, that's OK, then.' He hesitated. 'I wanted to ask your advice about a personal matter. You see, I met this girl. The day before the crash actually. She's English. And I thought that you, being an Englishwoman, would be able to advise me what to do.'

Sarah sat down on the chair at the side of Jack's bed. 'I'd like to help if I can but…'

'You see, Lauren was the waitress who brought the pizza to my table the night before my crash. I started to talk in English to her and we were getting on really well until her boss called her over. I managed to speak to her again just as I was leaving and we agreed to meet the next evening outside the pizzeria when she finished work.'

Giacomo leaned back against his pillows and gave a deep sigh before continuing. 'I don't expect she waited long but I would have liked to have got a message to her. It's too late now that I look like a freak.'

'It's never too late and you don't look like a freak!'

'So do you think I should try and contact her?'

'Jack, it's up to you. But you've got nothing to lose, have you?'

'I could write a letter to Lauren and send it to the pizzeria, couldn't I?'

Sarah smiled as she stood up. 'You could indeed. Now, I'll have to be getting back to Pronto Soccorso.'

'Thanks for making my mind up for me.'

'Good luck!'

*   *   *

'Carlos was looking for you a few minutes ago,' Lucia told her when she got back. He's just gone back to his office.'

Sarah glanced at her watch. She should have been off duty an hour ago.

'I'll call in and see what he wants.'

Carlos looked up and smiled when she went in.

'Sarah. I was just about to bleep you.'

'I'm off duty.' She sank down into a chair.

Carlos stood up and came round the desk. 'I know you're off duty. So am I, theoretically. If I don't get out of here soon, somebody will ask me to do something. I was wondering if you'd like to have dinner with me.'

Sarah smiled. 'I'd love to have dinner. I didn't have time for lunch and I'm absolutely starving.'

'Good! I don't mean good that you're starving, but good that you'll have dinner with me. You need feeding up. You're too thin. I'm sure you've got thinner this week. You need another two or three kilos.'

Sarah gave a hoarse laugh. How ironic!

'Oh, I expect I could manage that, if I worked on it.'

'Promise!'

'No problem. There's just one request about tonight...' Sarah paused as she looked up at Carlos.

'*Si?*'

Carlos was looking down at her with a heart-rending smile. He'd already shaken off his professional persona and was a completely different character to the medical boss he'd been this morning when he'd chided her about her punctuality. She recognised the hot-blooded Carlos she'd had a crush on when she'd been a teenager. Fun-loving, adventurous, ready for any experience...

She knew she had to concentrate on the present situation and not get too carried away by nostalgic memories that would hinder her intention of maintaining their comfortable platonic relationship.

'Carlos, I don't want to go anywhere posh tonight. I'd like to eat quickly in some little—'

'Eat quickly! In Roma?' Carlos put both hands on her shoulders and looked deeply into her eyes. His mouth was twitching.

Sarah grinned. 'Don't look so scandalised. And don't scold me either. The last time you looked like that was when I knocked over that bottle of red wine on the white tablecloth at your twentieth birthday party. I'm very hungry now and if I don't eat something quickly I'll…' She broke off.

Carlos was now looking down at her with a tender concern. 'I know the very place,' he said gently. 'We can walk there in five minutes. It's very informal…and very quick.'

He took hold of her hand and led her to the door. She looked down at her white coat.

'Do I need to change?'

Carlos shrugged. 'You can wear what you like at this *enoteca*. It's an unpretentious wine bar that serves food. Simply take off your white coat…here, let me help you. Go and get that warm coat you wore the other evening and you're ready.'

'We're going to walk along the side of the river and it can be chilly at this time of the year,' Carlos told her a few minutes later as they went out through the front entrance of the hospital.

Sarah noticed that Carlos was wearing an overcoat over his suit. He took hold of her gloved hand as he led her to the pedestrian bridge that crossed the busy road. The path along the side of the river was well lit. Couples were lingering beside the water at the beginning of an evening out. An illuminated boat floated by. It was all very romantic, especially with Carlos holding her hand.

She wondered if holding hands was affecting him as much as it was her. Was it usual for platonic friends to hold hands? Maybe Carlos simply thought it was practical so that he could help her along the areas she was unfamiliar with. If anyone saw them now they would assume they were a couple, whereas they were simply…she had no idea what they were! Their present relationship was too complex to analyse while her insides were demanding food—anything, bread or milk or—

'We're here!'

'Thank heaven!' she breathed as she looked up at the illuminated sign. ENOTECA GIOVANNI.

'It's an informal wine bar owned by Giovanni,' Carlos said, putting an arm in the small of her back to guide her through the door.

Inside, the atmosphere was warm, crowded and inviting. A small, rotund man with black side whiskers, wearing a white apron over his striped black trousers, came bustling towards them with his hand outstretched.

'*Buona sera, Dottore Fellini.*'

'*Buona sera, Giovanni. Ha un tavolo per due?*'

'Of course I have a table for you, Dottore. Come this way.'

Giovanni led them to a table by the window overlooking the river. A young couple were lingering over their coffee. Giovanni spoke quietly to them. The couple immediately smiled and stood up, making their way to the bar.

'I hope we didn't inconvenience those two,' Sarah said as she sat down. 'I couldn't hear what Giovanni was saying to them but it certainly made them leave in a hurry.'

Carlos smiled. 'Giovanni offered them a free drink at the bar if they would vacate their table for an important client and his beautiful lady.'

Sarah leaned back against her chair and looked across at Giovanni. 'You Italians are so gallant. I feel anything but beautiful tonight. I haven't even had a shower or changed out of this working skirt and blouse I've been wearing all day.'

Carlos stretched out his hand to grasp hers. 'You look beautiful to me, Sarah.'

The touch of his fingers was electric. She would have to tell him soon that she was pregnant. She couldn't keep him in the dark, pretending to be somebody she wasn't. But not yet... Tonight she was enjoying his attentions too much! This was a side of Carlos she'd never seen when they'd just been good friends. He was flirting with her now and she loved it.

A waiter was whisking away the tablecloth used by the young couple and replacing it with a clean red and white gingham one. The candle in the bottle was being replaced because too much wax was dripping onto the tablecloth.

Sarah sighed as she looked around her. It was a romantic sort of place. A place for lovers to spend the evening. Maybe she could go on pretending a little while longer... Just for tonight or...?

'Why are you smiling in that mischievous way, Sarah?'

She laughed. 'Private thoughts. If I told you...'

'Go on! Be a sport, as you English say. Tell me.'

'Later...perhaps. First I need food to gather my strength.'

Quickly, she picked up the menu. Her mouth was positively salivating as she ran her eyes down the list of dishes. Without looking up, she stretched her hand towards the glass of bread sticks in the centre of the table and chewed hungrily.

'I'd like *spaghetti alla carbonara*, which is always fantastic in Rome. And a green salad and perhaps some *bruschetta* to eat while we wait,' she said, putting down the menu.

The *bruschetta* appeared on the table very quickly and Sarah hungrily devoured a piece. As the hunger pangs began to disappear she felt much safer. She wasn't going to disgrace herself by having to dash to the loo because she was feeling sick!

She was deliberately not taking any medication for the nausea she felt most mornings and at other times during the day, usually when she was hungry. Having read about the disastrous effects of thalidomide, the anti-nausea pill given to pregnant women in the early 1960s, she'd decided not to risk anything. Most pregnant women found the nausea disappeared after the first three months.

'You always liked *bruschetta*, I remember,' Carlos said, handing over the plate towards Sarah so that she could take another piece.

'I sometimes used to make my own version in London. Toast some bread, rub it with salt, garlic and olive oil. Then I'd add some tomatoes. Delicious!'

'You're enjoying that, aren't you? You must have been very hungry.'

'I was, but I'm feeling much better.'

Carlos sipped his wine. It was an excellent Chianti Classico that he'd wanted Sarah to try, but so far she hadn't touched her glass.

'Tell me about your life in London. What happened to that boyfriend you were living with? What was his name? You did tell me about a year ago but I've forgotten.'

Sarah swallowed her second piece of *bruschetta* before wiping her hands on a red and white check napkin.

'Oh, Robin and I decided to split up. It was all perfectly amicable. We both decided we wanted to have a change from London. Robin's gone off to Africa with a French medical aid group.'

'And no hard feelings on either side? There's usually some kind of animosity between couples when they split.'

'Like I said, perfectly amicable,' she said quickly.

The spaghetti had arrived. It looked extremely tempting and she could see that the chef had been generous with the bacon, eggs and cheese mixed in with the spaghetti. Just how she liked it.

She swallowed a couple of delicious mouthfuls before continuing their conversation.

'I gather your situation's changed as well, Carlos. You were sharing an apartment with somebody a couple of years ago, I remember.'

Carlos speared a piece of fish on the end of his fork. 'You mean Christina. Big mistake! It started out as a sharing arrangement. We got on well as friends and decided to split the rent on a flat. After a while we became lovers. Soon after that, Christina insisted I go to meet her family.'

Carlos rolled his eyes and Sarah laughed at his exaggerated expression of despair. At the same time she was trying to quell the unwelcome pangs of jealousy she was feeling for this Christina woman that Carlos had lived with.

Carlos leaned forward conspiratorially and lowered his voice. He glanced around the room, a mock expression of fear on his face, as if he was worried that someone might know who he was talking about.

'The mother was such an overpowering, dominant sort of woman. Almost as desperate as her daughter that there should be a wedding as soon as possible. Living together wasn't an option for either of them. I tell you, I was lucky to escape with my life from that relationship! We had absolutely nothing in common, Christina and I.'

'So you moved back into hospital accommodation?'

Carlos nodded. 'The safest place to be and the easiest lifestyle. I can do my job without worrying about domestic chores. And no travelling problems. One of these days...'

Carlos put down his fork and looked across the table. 'Some time in the future, when I've found somebody who...well, I'm sure it will happen if I take my time. Now, tell me about night life in London, plays you have seen, films you have enjoyed. Come on, Sarah, you must have led an interesting life in the big city. Am I right?'

Sarah searched her memory. As she outlined a few of the more interesting aspects of her off duty time, she realised that she'd been languishing in a social and cultural desert for too long. She and Robin hadn't made an effort to go to any of the excellent concerts at the Festival Hall or Albert Hall. There had been films she'd planned to see but in the end they'd waited until the video had become available and had watched it in the flat. But here in Rome with Carlos, everything was going to be different. Together, they would go to see all her favourite landmarks in Rome…

She stopped her train of thought even as it arose. She was making it all seem so easy, whereas there was the little matter of her pregnancy and then…and then her baby. Or even babies! She'd yet to face the possibility that she might be carrying twins, considering that they ran in her family!

'I'd like to finish with fresh fruit,' she said quickly. 'It's good for… It's good for me.'

'Of course. And then we'll have coffee and maybe a small glass of something to—'

'Not for me, Carlos. Coffee keeps me awake. And definitely no alcohol! I mean, thank you, Carlos but I daren't risk a hangover when I've got to work tomorrow.'

'But you haven't even touched your wine! You've certainly changed since the last time your parents invited me over to stay at your house. I remember your father taking everybody down to the village pub and—'

Sarah groaned. 'How can I forget? I was trying out the local beer for the first time and it wasn't a good idea.'

Carlos gave her a wry grin. 'I remember Lucy refused to touch it, but you always were the daring one, jumping in with both feet before anybody had explained the dangers. I used to think it was because Lucy was the elder sister that she was always more cautious than you.'

'Lucy's only ten minutes older than me!'

'Yes, but ten years wiser!'

Sarah grinned. 'How dare you say that? Even if it's true! I've always envied the way Lucy evaluates her every move.'

She leaned forward, elbows on the tablecloth, something she'd never been allowed to do as a child.

'You know, Carlos, when our grandmother died, she left Lucy and me her cottage in the Yorkshire Dales. I suggested we sell it because I was short of money. But Lucy had the cottage valued by an estate agent and asked if she could buy my share from me. I readily agreed. I needed the money for my London rent whereas Lucy planned to work in a hospital in Yorkshire when she finished medical school. The cottage is now worth at least twice as much as it was ten years ago and I've spent my share on renting a place.'

'But I expect you enjoyed your time in London, didn't you?'

Sarah smiled. 'I've tried my hardest to enjoy every minute but sometimes I've tried too hard. That's why I don't want a hangover tomorrow.'

'I'll get the bill.' Carlos raised his hand to a passing waiter.

It had started to rain so Carlos insisted on getting a taxi. 'You're looking tired again, Sarah.'

'I'm fine, but I don't fancy a walk in the rain.'

'Shall I try to arrange a day when we can both be off duty together so that we can see some of the interesting areas of Rome?' Carlos asked as they settled themselves in the back of a taxi.

'That would be great!'

Had Carlos been reading her thoughts? She'd hold off her revelations about the pregnancy until after their day out together. Just one more day of make-believe that they were becoming romantically involved and then she'd bite the bullet and confess.

'How about some time next week perhaps? You'd better check your diary.'

Sarah grinned. 'No need. I'm entirely at the mercy of my dictatorial boss. If he says work, I work. If he says play, I play. My life is as simple as that.'

'OK. I'll tell you exactly what day we can play together as soon as I've worked out everybody's schedule.'

Sarah looked out of the cab window at the rain bouncing off the paving stones at the side of the road. She didn't want anything to change between her and Carlos. She wanted the same kind of easy friendship to go on for...well, a little while longer. But something quite unpredictable had happened to her emotions this evening. She was beginning to think that she would love their friendship to progress into a full-blown romantic relationship.

She turned to look at Carlos. The lights from a passing car were illuminating his handsome, olive-skinned features, the strong, determined thrust of his chiselled jaw. She knew without a shadow of a doubt that she'd progressed beyond youthful adulation. She was falling in love.

But would Carlos want her if he knew she was pregnant? No chance! Trapped into a relationship with a woman who was having another man's child? It was far worse than his Christina scenario. At least his ex-girlfriend had only wanted Carlos to commit to marriage, whereas she herself came as a family package complete with all the problems of a pregnancy.

Would Carlos wait until she'd had her baby and...?

Carlos turned suddenly and saw her watching him. He leaned across and drew her closer to him.

'Why are you looking at me like that, Sarah?'

'Like what?'

'As if you needed to remember my face so that you could

paint it. Do you remember how you used to paint portraits on the side of old cardboard boxes and invite everybody to your exhibitions? You used to charge exorbitant entrance fees to your messy studio in the garden shed. You seemed to think it was necessary to cover yourself with paint as well as the cardboard boxes.'

'I'll have you know my exorbitant fees were always part of a fundraising campaign to help one of my mother's charities.'

'Oh, Sarah, my summers would have been so dull if you hadn't been there to liven things up!'

Carlos took her face in both his hands and kissed her gently on the lips. She lifted her fingers and entwined them in his hair, lovingly stroking the back of his head with a slow sensual movement.

The cab had lurched to a halt. Sarah pulled herself away and looked into Carlos's eyes. He appeared stunned at the impact of their embrace. They'd both wanted that to happen and it had nothing at all to do with nostalgia.

CHAPTER FOUR

CARLOS took hold of her hand as they turned the corner and began to walk down the corridor that led to the medical residents' quarters. Sarah entwined her fingers with his, luxuriating in the feel of his skin against hers. She'd deliberately removed her gloves as she'd left the taxi in the hope that they might soon hold hands.

Carlos had behaved with professional composure as they'd walked through the reception area, acknowledging the greetings of the night staff, but now that they were on neutral ground, almost at his room, Sarah could feel him relaxing.

All she wanted now at the end of their evening together was a kiss. Not a goodnight kiss from a platonic friend, but something a little more romantic. Nothing too prolonged because she knew that within the near future she would be forced to reveal the truth and then all hopes of a real affair would be dashed. But just for tonight she wanted to prolong the excitement of discovering they were something more than just good friends.

During the last week, she'd made a point of finding out which room was Carlos's. They were getting very near now. She would enjoy a slow, sensual kiss with Carlos but then she would hurry away back to her room.

That was what she intended until she heard him say, 'Would you like to come in for a coffee? Oh, I forgot, you don't drink coffee this late, do you?'

Carlos was slotting his key in the lock. The door swung open. He turned to look at her. Was it her imagination or did he look nervous? Was he as scared of upsetting the balance of their friendship as she was?

The temptation to prolong the evening was too much for her.

'I'd like a glass of mineral water,' she said quickly. 'I'm very thirsty.'

She had to seize this opportunity because once she'd made her fateful announcement there would be no more opportunities for a drink and a chat at the end of a romantic evening together. She may never even get the chance to see inside Carlos's room if she didn't go in this evening.

'Your place is much bigger than mine,' she said as she followed Carlos into the small kitchen. 'And I don't have the luxury of a separate kitchen. I've just got a cafetière and a small hotplate in the corner of the bedroom.'

Carlos reached into the fridge for a bottle of mineral water and poured some into a glass. He poured himself a cognac before leading Sarah back into the main living room.

Sarah sank down on to the sofa and sipped her water as she looked around her. The door to the bedroom was partially open. She moved to the edge of the sofa and leaned forward so that she could get a better view.

'You can go and have a look in the bedroom if you want,' Carlos said, his mouth twitching with amusement. 'You always were inquisitive.'

Sarah pulled a wry face. 'Oh, I'm far too grown up now to go and inspect your bedroom.'

Carlos put down his drink and moved closer, his eyes full of deep tenderness as he watched her.

'Oh, I don't know,' he said huskily. 'I would say you've reached the perfect age to go and inspect my bedroom.'

He drew her against him, running his fingers through her hair as his lips touched hers in a long, tenderly gentle kiss. Slowly, with such exquisite sensitivity of touch, he caressed the soft skin at the nape of her neck. His hand strayed across her bare shoulders, moving slowly downwards to cup one of her breasts in a tantalisingly erotic movement that made Sarah shiver with anticipation.

She could feel desire, the longing for fulfilment mounting inside her. She'd learned from her medical research that women still felt sexy when they were pregnant, but she hadn't realised she would feel as impossibly, erotically aroused as she did now. But she couldn't allow Carlos to make love to her! Not now when…

'Carlos, there's something I have to tell you. I—'

'No, let me speak first,' he said, taking her face in his hands, placing one gentle finger over her lips. 'I never in a million years thought I would ever feel like this about you. To me, you've always been just Sarah, my little Sarah, but now—'

'No, Carlos!'

As Sarah pulled herself away, she saw the puzzled look in Carlos's eyes.

'I'm sorry, Sarah, I thought you wanted to make love. You seemed so—'

'I wanted you to kiss me. But I…'

She stood up and moved quickly towards the door. 'I must go before… I can't stay any longer.'

Carlos reached the door before she did, standing with his back against it as he looked down at her with concerned eyes.

'I did not mean to offend you.' His Italian accent was stronger than usual as he struggled to find the correct English words. 'It was too soon. Perhaps another time when—'

'You didn't offend me, Carlos, but please don't talk about the future. Let's just live in the present until after we've had our day out together. After that we'll talk. I'll explain why I'm being so difficult.'

A look of relief flooded his eyes. 'Oh, so you still want to spend the day with me?'

'Of course I do!'

She reached up and kissed him on his cheek. 'Goodnight, Carlos. Thank you for a wonderful evening.'

Carlos went into the kitchen and poured himself another drink after Sarah had gone. For the life of him he didn't know what to make of Sarah at the moment! One minute she was coming on to him, the next she was pushing him away. He'd never imagined he'd ever find himself falling in love with her, but it had just happened and there wasn't a thing he could do about it.

Leaning against the table, swirling the ice around in his glass, he tried to analyse what had gone wrong this evening. He should have waited until he was really sure of Sarah's feelings before he'd kissed her in that suggestive way. He'd made it too obvious that he was hoping to carry her off to his bedroom if that was what she wanted.

But from the way she'd snuggled up to him in the taxi, the way she'd clung to him when he'd started to kiss her, the way she'd caressed him... She'd even sighed and moaned as if she wanted more, much more! Undeniably, she'd seemed to be trying hard to keep herself in control, but he'd thought that had been simply because she'd wanted him to take the lead.

He took a long gulp of his drink. *Mamma mia!* What on earth was a man to think? He wasn't made of stone!

With any other woman he would have felt angry to have been led on like that. But his affection for Sarah had only deepened because of it. He'd always respected her and he realised that she must have some reason for escaping from their passionate embrace just when they were really getting to know each other in this new, exciting relationship he was enjoying so much.

'Oh, Sarah, Sarah...!'

He put his head in his hands and groaned. If only she'd stayed with him tonight! He would have convinced her there was no problem in making the transition from friends to lovers.

Back in her room, Sarah stretched out on the bed, peeling off her clothes. She was too exhausted even to drag herself into the shower. What should have been the perfect ending to a wonderful evening had ended in disaster. Well, perhaps disaster was an exaggeration. But she knew now that she shouldn't have gone into Carlos's room. She shouldn't have led him on as she had. The sooner she told him the truth the easier it would be for both of them.

But not until they'd had their day out together! She wanted at least to have the memories of that one day before she took her pregnancy completely seriously, before she started getting fatter and completely unfanciable, before she grew up and had to put another tiny human being's needs before her own.

As she patted her abdomen, she felt a strange feeling coming over her. Was she actually beginning to bond with her baby? Finding out that she was pregnant had been so traumatic that all she'd been able to think about were the problems a baby would bring to her life. Was she beginning to realise that she might actually enjoy being a mother? That motherhood wouldn't simply be a dutiful commitment?

'I'm sorry, little one,' she whispered. 'You didn't ask to be born into an uncertain situation. I do love you, really I do. And I'm going to be a good mother to you.'

She stretched out and grabbed a tissue as she felt the tears pricking behind her eyelids. Talking to her baby like this was comforting. Motherhood didn't seem quite so scary.

'One day you'll understand why I haven't told anybody

yet. I'm still hanging onto the old life I knew with Carlos. I love him so much and I wish he was your daddy but you can't always have what you want in this life. You'll know soon enough what I'm talking about, especially if you're a girl. But for now, just be patient. I'll put you first from now on.'

She reached for the bedside light and turned it off. In the semi-darkness of the twinkling lights of the cars and ambulances driving in and out of the hospital forecourt and the constant hum of the traffic down on the riverside road she began to feel calm enough to fall asleep.

It was nearly two weeks before Carlos told Sarah that he'd organised a whole day off duty for the pair of them.

Sarah had begun to think Carlos had abandoned the idea—and who could blame him, considering the way she'd behaved the last time he'd taken her out? As she dressed that morning, in warm trousers, sweater and her big winter coat, she felt decidedly nervous and apprehensive about the day ahead. She was simply going to enjoy seeing a few of the sights with Carlos and then, at the end of their excursion, as they sat in a *trattoria*, she'd tell him she was pregnant.

She'd no idea how he would react. She'd gone over it so many times in her own mind. He would be shocked, of course, and then he'd realise that they would have to go back to being just friends again. She hoped he wouldn't be angry and suggest she go back to England. The worst scenario would be if she lost his friendship altogether.

But for today she simply wanted to be with Carlos, to enjoy being near him, to pretend that there were no problems looming on her personal horizon.

'Where are we going from here?' she asked Carlos as he held open the taxi door so that she could get out. 'This is the Piazza Venezia, isn't it?'

'That's right. I thought it would be interesting to walk along to the Forum, explore that for an hour or so before climbing up the Capitoline Hill to the temple of Jupiter.'

'Excellent! I used to love exploring the ruins of the Forum.'

Carlos guided her past the entrance to the Piazza Venezia museum. 'We haven't time to go in there today. We'll go back another time.'

'I remember spending what seemed like hours in there with my father when I was small. There was a thirteenth-century gilded angel that took my fancy. I stood in front of it for ages when I heard how old it was. Absolutely fascinating! I'd love to go in and see it again, but today I want to spend as much time in the fresh air as possible. I've spent too long cooped up in hospital this week.'

'Rome is always cold at this time of year, but if we keep moving, we'll be OK.'

Sarah looked up at the sky. A pale winter sun was trying to peep through the clouds.

'It's cold, but there's a promise of spring in the air, Carlos.'

He touched her cold cheek and smiled. 'Ever the optimist, aren't you?'

'I hope so! I'm going to need all my optimism soon.'

'What's that suppose to mean?'

'Oh…I'll tell you later.'

They rounded the corner from the museum and Sarah looked up at the ornate façade of the church of San Marco.

'I seem to remember going in there with my parents and Lucy. And you were there as well, weren't you, Carlos?'

Carlos nodded. 'Yes, your parents invited me to come up to Rome from the coast on a family outing one summer. I remember showing you that beautiful ninth-century mosaic. You stared at it for ages, completely still and quiet for once. I told you it was very old and you asked if it was older than your grandmother.'

Sarah laughed. 'I don't remember saying that, but I do remember the strange smell in San Marco.'

'Incense. You walked around holding your nose until your mother asked me if I would take you outside for some fresh air.'

'You were very patient with me, Carlos.'

'I'm always patient with you, Sarah.' He paused and looked down at her with a tender expression. 'I can wait until the end of the day for you to tell me whatever it is that's worrying you. You promised we'd have a discussion, remember?'

'I remember,' she said, quietly as she suppressed a shiver. 'Come on, let's walk. I feel chilly standing still.'

Carlos took hold of her hand. She quickened her pace to fit in with his long strides. She wasn't allowing herself to think about the end of the day. The present moment was all important. She would cope with this evening and the sleepless night that would follow when the time arose.

She enjoyed exploring the Forum, visiting many of her favourite sections before climbing the zig-zag path that led to the ruins of the Capitol, the Temple of Jupiter.

'Strange to think the temple was the most important in ancient Rome,' Carlos said as they began to walk around the site.

'I remember it was built about 500 BC, wasn't it?'

Carlos flicked over the page of his well thumbed guide book. 'Five hundred and nine BC according to this. It was about as big as the Pantheon.'

'Very impressive! I'm fascinated by old things.'

Carlos gave her a wry grin. 'Does that include me?'

Sarah smiled. 'You're not old enough. You're still only thirty-eight. October, your birthday, isn't it?'

'What a memory! And yours is July if I'm not mistaken. The big three-O.'

'Don't remind me!' She stopped walking and took a deep breath. 'Any chance of some lunch around here? I'm—'

'Don't tell me, I know. You're starving again. I think that's enough culture for the moment,' Carlos said, taking her hand as they went down the *cordonata*, the magnificent steps created by Michelangelo.

They walked along the Via del Teatro di Marcello back towards the Piazza Venezia.

'There's a small restaurant I've visited a couple of times in a street near here,' Carlos said. 'I can't remember the name of the street but... There it is, along here, Sarah.'

He held open the door. The warmth and the delicious smell of cooking was very inviting. They were shown to a corner table. Even though it was lunchtime there were candles on the tables. The room was small, cosy and infinitely romantic.

Sarah looked around her, soaking up the romantic atmosphere. At any other time in her life she would have loved this place. But the thought that she had to break up their budding romantic relationship before it went any further was making her apprehensive.

Carlos was ordering a bottle of champagne and a bottle of mineral water.

'You can drink whichever you prefer,' he said casually. 'I know what I'm having.'

'I'd like a glass of champagne, Carlos.'

Unconsciously, she placed her hand beneath her napkin over her tummy as if to comfort her baby. She was trying to send a message to her baby, telling her—or him, but probably her—that Mummy's one glass of champagne wouldn't be harmful. And it might give Mummy some false courage for what she had to tell Carlos this evening.

Carlos leaned across the table and took hold of her hand. 'What are you smiling about?'

'Nothing important! Just…private thoughts.'

'You've had a lot of private thoughts recently.' He gave her a wry smile. 'There's something going on, isn't there?'

'We agreed to talk about it tonight, Carlos.'

'I didn't agree to anything. You told me that you would—Oh, *grazie*…'

Carlos took the menu that the waiter was holding out.

Sarah managed to steer the conversation on to safer ground as they enjoyed a simple light lunch of *tagliatelle*, followed by fresh fruit.

At the end of the meal, Carlos said he'd like to go to the Piazza di Spagna.

'There's an art exhibition in the Villa Medici that I think you'd enjoy.'

A couple of hours later as they emerged from the Villa Medici, Sarah suggested they sit on the Spanish Steps for a short time to soak up the welcome winter sunshine.

'I know it's winter but I always sit on the steps and so do all the other tourists.'

She waved her arm to point out the large number of people sprawled around the wide stone steps, their faces uplifted towards the elusive sun.

'Yes, but you're not a tourist. You live here now.'

She smiled. 'Makes no difference. I love the view of the city from here.'

Carlos squatted on the steps beside her. 'You haven't changed one bit, Sarah,' he said, his voice tender.

Sarah swallowed hard, unable to comment on that. Carlos took hold of her hand. The touch of his fingers was, oh, so comforting but also unnerving.

'Come on, let's walk!' She jumped to her feet. 'Would you mind if we went shopping around the Via Condotti? I really need some leather boots for my poor little cold feet and you might find some shoes for yourself, Carlos.'

'You know how I love shopping!' he said wryly.

'Oh, Carlos! *Per favore!*'

He raised his hands in the air as he saw her disappointed look. '*Mamma mia!* Don't worry! I will come with you and carry your packages. We have experienced enough Roman culture for one day.'

'That was a most successful shopping trip,' Sarah said as Carlos loaded their packages into the boot of the taxi. 'I love my new boots!'

'We bought too many things,' Carlos said, holding open the door for Sarah to climb in.

'Yes, but it was fun, wasn't it?' Sarah said as she climbed in the back of the cab.

Carlos joined her on the back seat. 'No comment, as you English say! But tell me, why did you buy that enormous jacket? I told you it was two sizes too big for you.'

'Yes, but I can wear it with a belt to cinch in the waist. And they didn't have a smaller size.'

Carlos was leaning forward to speak to the driver, giving him directions.

'Where are we going?' Sarah asked.

'I've got to check on my parents' apartment. They're down on the coast for a couple of weeks. One of the houses has been vacated and they're supervising some refurbishment. I told them I couldn't get away from the hospital at the moment but I promised to keep an eye on their apartment here in Rome.'

'I haven't been there since I was small. I remember it's very posh, isn't it? Loads of antiques you mustn't touch, especially if you've got sticky fingers, and precious chairs you mustn't climb on.'

She switched to Italian as the memories flooded back. 'Take your shoes off at the door, Sarah!'

Carlos laughed at Sarah's excellent imitation of his mother's voice. He remembered she'd always been a brilliant mimic. That was one reason why she had such a good Italian accent.

The taxi was drawing up in front of the prestigious apartment block in the quiet residential street.

'It looks just as I remember it,' Sarah said, as she walked up the immaculate carpet from the front lobby where the uniformed porter had clicked his heels to attention, saluting Carlos as if he were a visiting general reviewing the troops.

Carlos unlocked the heavy oak door, dumped his armful of packages on the highly polished floor of the hall before helping Sarah unload the parcels she was carrying. She slipped her aching feet out of her shoes and made for the nearest sofa where she stretched out amongst the squashy cushions.

Carlos brought her the glass of mineral water she'd requested. She felt extremely thirsty. That was another of the symptoms she often experienced.

'Thanks, Carlos.'

She drank half of it before she put the glass down on the table beside her. She was especially careful that it was placed on a protective coaster so as not to spoil the antique surface of the table. The euphoria she'd experienced from her glass of champagne at lunchtime had evaporated. The false courage she'd hoped for wasn't going to happen.

She'd better get it over with. The longer she procrastinated the worse it would be. Carlos was still busying himself with the packages.

'Carlos, when are you going to sit down so we can talk?'

'I'm coming!'

He sat down on the other end of the sofa. Sarah looked across at him and, apprehensive as she was, she felt a pang of desire. The tenderness in his eyes was almost too much to bear, considering what she was about to tell him. Could she hold out any longer? If only she could prolong the wonderful rapport that existed between them. Carlos was her soul-mate. She loved him so much and because of that she had to come clean.

She cleared her throat. 'Carlos, there's something...'

But he was moving along the sofa with smooth, fluid, sexy movements of his muscular body. She waited as he took hold of her hands, tenderly caressing the palms until she could feel her resolution beginning to evaporate.

'Sarah, before you start telling me your problems, I've got an idea to put to you. We don't have to go back to hospital tonight. I'd like to spend the evening here. I'll cook supper and—'

'Carlos...'

'Yes, what is it, darling?'

He'd never called her darling before. His voice was husky, too sexy for her to listen to at this fateful moment. She held her breath as he drew her against him, kissing her gently on the lips, tenderly caressing her until, too late, she realised that her wanton body was reacting to his electric touch.

She ought to pull away now before she became any more aroused. She had to ignore the frissons of desire that were running down her spine. But that now familiar feeling of liquid desire that arose from deep down inside her whenever Carlos touched her was claiming her senses. Her body was taking over, demanding to be satisfied. She was losing herself again to the magic power Carlos held over her...

As he kissed her she closed her eyes in absolute bliss, losing all the inhibitions she'd tried to fix firmly in place. Her brain registered that Carlos had just suggested they stay here for the evening. If they stayed for the evening she knew she would want to remain in his arms all night, and she couldn't! She simply couldn't prolong the delicious agony of wanting him desperately any longer.

Time was running out. She mustn't go on pretending that she was free to make love because…

'I'm pregnant!' She pulled herself away as she cried out.

Carlos recoiled and stared at her. 'What did you say?'

She took a deep breath. 'I'm pregnant. About eight, nearly nine weeks.'

He sat up, running a hand through his tousled hair. 'Are you sure?'

She nodded. 'Completely sure.'

He looked utterly perplexed. 'But when did you realise that…?'

She turned away so that she couldn't see the look of dismay in his eyes. She wanted to say that she'd just found out, but she couldn't. He deserved a straight answer.

'I found out soon after I left England. On the plane actually.'

'On the plane!' Carlos stood up and started pacing around the room.

'I did a pregnancy test. It was positive.'

Carlos opened the window, leaning out to take a few deep breaths. He felt as if he was drowning. Drowning in a nightmare.

With his back towards her, Sarah couldn't tell whether he was angry, disappointed or simply in a state of shock. She remained absolutely still and quiet, allowing him to consider her devastating news. After a while he seemed to recover his composure as he closed the window and returned to the sofa, standing, arms folded, looking down at her.

'But why didn't you tell me before?'

His voice was calm and quiet but she could tell that he was devastated.

She looked up at him. 'Carlos, I was playing for time,

allowing myself a brief interlude to settle into my new job before I had to tell you I was pregnant. I needed to come to terms with my own feelings. It had been a complete shock to me and initially I wasn't sure what I was going to do. Then, in the days that followed, I...'

She broke off. There was no point now in telling Carlos that after she'd fallen in love with him she'd wanted to enjoy a brief period of romance before she broke the news that was to change everything.

'And after that first day?' he prompted, as he sat down beside her on the sofa. 'Why couldn't you tell me in the days that followed? You've had nearly three weeks.'

She turned to face him. 'I was enjoying our...our new friendship. Our adult friendship that seemed to have all the promise of... Well, we were having such fun together, weren't we? I didn't want to spoil it.'

'Yes, we were having fun,' he said quietly.

She swallowed hard as she noted the emphasis he'd placed on the word 'were', making it quite plain their fun was now all in the past.

'Whose baby is it?'

'It's Robin's.'

He moved away to the other end of the sofa. 'But I thought your relationship was over!'

'It was! We'd split up but...' Sarah took a deep breath. This was the bit she was really dreading!

'Robin came back to the flat a couple of weeks before Christmas to pick up some of the stuff he'd left behind. He was on his way to a party and he had a couple of bottles of champagne with him. He decided to open one of the bottles so we could celebrate the fact that we'd both got the jobs we wanted.'

She stood up and walked over to the window. From this first-floor window she had a good view of the street below. A bejewelled lady in an expensive coat was being escorted towards a waiting cab by a tall, distinguished-looking man in a dinner jacket. They moved together as if they had a lifetime of memories behind them. The man's hand was in the small of his wife's back as he helped her into the cab.

That sort of mellow relationship took time to develop. They'd probably got a loving family of devoted children, all born under the umbrella of a happy marriage. Whereas she herself hadn't even got a father for her unborn child! She'd completely messed up her life and that of her poor little daughter who was going to be born into...

She was aware that Carlos was standing behind her. She could feel his breath against the back of her hair. She turned quickly and found herself closer than she'd imagined. She looked up and saw that his eyes were deeply troubled.

'So, when Robin arrived with the champagne, was that the evening when you fell pregnant?' he asked evenly. 'Or did he come back before Christmas so that—?'

'Please, Carlos. Don't make it sound so... It was just that one evening. It shouldn't have happened, I know, but—'

'Sarah, I'm not being judgmental!' Carlos moved along to place both hands on either side of her shoulders. 'I've made mistakes in relationships, too. Who hasn't? But...it's just that I never imagined you would... How did it happen that you fell pregnant? I mean, weren't you on the Pill or anything?'

She shook her head. 'I was on the Pill when Robin and I lived together. But when we split up I stopped taking it. That night...it's all so hazy...I'd forgotten I wasn't on the Pill. Something in the familiar setting of Robin and me being together again in the flat where we'd lived together had temporarily thrown me off balance and... Oh, Carlos, don't make me go on...'

Carlos knew he had no intention of dwelling on the details of Sarah's fateful encounter with her ex-boyfriend. It was too traumatic for him to even contemplate another man making love to Sarah. He was utterly consumed with jealousy of this unknown man called Robin. If he came face to face with him now he would like to… But that wouldn't solve anything. He had to think clearly. This man was the father of Sarah's unborn child and therefore had family rights.

He tightened his grip on Sarah's shoulders. She shivered at the touch of his fingers. If only he would take her in his arms now and tell her that he didn't mind the fact she was carrying another man's child, that it didn't make any difference to…

'Sarah, my main concern now is for your welfare,' Carlos said eventually.

Sarah swallowed hard as she looked up at the impassive expression on Carlos's face. He'd spoken in the same tone of voice he sometimes used to his patients, especially the ones who were being difficult and uncooperative.

'Carlos, you don't have to worry about me. This is my problem. I'm happy to be a single parent. I want this baby and—'

'Of course! But have you taken any steps to get antenatal care?'

'Not yet! I'm only two months pregnant, for heaven's sake! Some women don't even known they're pregnant at this stage.'

'Yes, but you're a doctor!' he said, in a steely voice.

He ran a hand through his dark hair and turned away, walking over to the ornate marble fireplace.

Looking at him now, standing under the portrait of his aristocratic-looking grandfather, Sarah realised just how much she loved him and how much she'd now lost. If only Carlos were the father of her baby! If only her baby would going to be born into a stable, loving family. As a single mother, she was going to devote her life to her daughter but a secure family background would have been so much better.

Carlos tapped his fingers against the fireplace. 'What about Robin? What does he think about being a father?'

'I haven't told him yet. I—'

'You haven't told him?'

Sarah cleared her throat nervously. 'I've been planning to phone him but I wanted to tell you first.'

'Why? I would have thought the father had a right to know first.'

'I know I should have made the effort to contact Robin,' she said quietly. 'But there has been so much going on during the three weeks I've known I was pregnant. And I wanted to be absolutely sure what was best for the baby and me before I told Robin.'

'Why?'

'Because I have no idea how Robin will react! He's very unpredictable. He always said he didn't want children but he might change his mind if he knew a child was on the way. He could even suggest we get back together for the sake of the child!'

'And how would you feel about that?' Carlos said, trying desperately to stifle the pangs of jealousy he felt towards this man who had stolen everything he had started to hope might be his.

'I would have to say no to the idea,' she said quietly.

Carlos was trying to ignore his own feelings as his strong sense of family values exerted itself. 'But in the interests of the child, don't you think that—?'

'No, Carlos. I know I can be a good mother to my baby on my own. I've had three weeks to think the situation through.'

'I think you should contact Robin as soon as possible. If it were my baby I'd have wanted to know immediately you found out!'

'Yes, but it's not your baby!'

She broke off. She'd hurt Carlos enough. He was only trying to help. She went across to the fireplace, putting up her hand to touch the side of Carlos's face. He remained totally still, as if not registering the fact that she was standing close to him. His expression was impassive as he stared down at her.

'I'm going to go back to hospital now,' she said. 'I hope we can be friends in the future but if you want me to go back to England I'll—'

'Of course I don't want you to go back to England!' He grabbed her hand, breathing quickly. 'Not unless you want to go back.'

'I don't,' she said. 'I love my work. I can work until just before the baby is due and then—'

'I don't think you should work longer than thirty-two weeks,' Carlos said, firmly. 'Not in Accident and Emergency. It's too dangerous. In fact, I won't allow it.'

'Carlos, with respect, this is my baby and—'

'And I'm in charge of A and E and I don't want my staff taking risks with their health. You can take maternity leave eight weeks before the baby is due and return when… You do want to return, don't you?'

'Of course I do. Why do you ask?'

'Well, you ought to consult Robin first.'

'I intend to. Carlos, I really want my baby.' She put her hands over her abdomen in an unconsciously defensive manner. 'I've thought everything through. Nothing's going to change in my work. I'm not going to be a liability in the department if that's what you're thinking.'

Carlos sighed. 'I'm not thinking anything at the moment,' he said in a dispirited voice. 'I feel utterly shocked. I can't believe this is happening to us.'

'Carlos, this is happening to me. You don't need to worry about it.'

'But I can't help worrying!'

He reached out towards her. She longed to rush into his arms but she didn't want his sympathy. She wanted his love. Love of a kind that he shouldn't lavish on someone who was carrying another man's child.

She turned away. 'I'm going back to hospital now. I'll call a cab on my mobile and—'

'I'm coming with you.'

She swung round. 'But I thought you had things to check on here at the apartment.'

He put a hand on her arm as if to detain her. 'Nothing that can't wait. It's more important I get you back to your room safely tonight. In your present state—'

'Carlos, I'm two months pregnant, that's all!'

'Yes, but you're in a highly emotional state at the moment and—'

'I'm not highly emotional!'

'Exactly! I rest my case.'

'Stop treating me like a child!'

'Stop behaving like one!'

Carlos reached for her coat and held it out in front of her. 'Put this on. I don't want you to catch cold. It's a cold evening. I'll phone for a taxi.'

She stood outside her room, waiting for Carlos to unlock her door. All the way back in the taxi he hadn't spoken to her. He'd simply sat there, staring straight ahead in stony silence. As the door swung open he reached down to pick up the packages he'd dumped on the floor. Without going into her room, he pushed them through the doorway. Then he bent his head and brushed her cheek with his lips.

The gesture was so impersonal she wanted to cry out with frustration. Take me in your arms! Tell me nothing has changed. Tell me you'll wait for me until I've had the baby...

'Goodnight, Sarah,' Carlos said solemnly. 'Take care of yourself. You can phone down to the canteen if you're hungry. They'll bring something to your room. And if you don't feel well in the morning, phone me and I'll—'

'Thank you, Carlos, I'll be fine. Goodnight.'

She closed the door and went slowly over to her bed. As she gently eased herself down onto the duvet, the tears she'd been holding back began to run down her cheeks. Quickly she grabbed a tissue. She wasn't going to give in to self-pity. That wasn't a trait she wanted her daughter to inherit.

Babies in the womb were sensitive to mood swings in their mothers. She mustn't dwell on her unhappiness at losing Carlos. She hoped she hadn't lost his friendship. After her baby was born, maybe Carlos might want to rekindle their romance. It was a significant maybe! A most unlikely maybe.

But in the meantime she had to concentrate on being a good mother to her unborn baby. She didn't want her child to pick up on the unhappy vibes she was experiencing.

She put her hand on her abdomen. It was still flat but cocooned in the warmth of her womb was a tiny foetus.

'I'm sorry about today,' she said gently. 'I hope I didn't upset you too much. We're going to be OK, you and me, honestly. I've decided I'd like to call you Charlotte. That's after my grandmother, your great-grandmother. She was a lovely lady and she'd be really pleased to have a great-granddaughter named after her. Charlotte if you're a girl, but if you turn out to be a boy I'll call you Charles, or I suppose I could call you Carlos, couldn't I? Perhaps not! Somehow I don't think Carlos would approve.'

She plumped up her pillows and leaned back against them. 'I suppose I could call you Charlie until I know for sure whether you're a girl or a boy.'

*   *   *

Back in his room, Carlos sank down on the sofa, picking up a cushion and punching his fist into the middle of it. That's what he'd like to do to Robin! How dare he go to Sarah's flat and make her pregnant? Perhaps Sarah hadn't exactly pushed him away. That made him feel even more unhappy. But the wretched man had plied her with drink and then taken advantage of her in her inebriated state, hadn't he?

And now Sarah was carrying Robin's child. The thought made him feel ill. He wished she'd told him when she'd first arrived, but then they wouldn't have had this little honeymoon. Honeymoon was an exaggeration of what had happened between them. But it had been so unexpected. To fall in love with Sarah would have been impossible to imagine a few years ago.

And just when it was going so well, she had to drop this bombshell. He didn't know what to think about their future relationship. At the moment his main feelings for Sarah were protective and caring. But at the same time he couldn't deny the fact that he still found her desirable. Pregnant or not, he was still deeply attracted to her.

He remembered how he'd planned the romantic seduction scenario for this evening. He'd been so sure that Sarah would want to make love with him. She'd been so warm, so sexily vibrant, so aroused, so…

He groaned. It was totally unthinkable now! She was carrying another man's child. The situation had completely changed and he didn't know how he would possibly come to terms with it.

But he was going to make sure that Sarah took care of herself. He felt he had a duty to look after her and her unborn, unplanned child. He would support her, whatever happened. But if the father turned up, he would have to keep himself in the background and relinquish his duties.

He sighed. If he was totally honest with himself, he realised that it would be in Sarah's and the baby's best interests if Robin shouldered his responsibilities and made a home for them. Family was everything. Robin was the father of Sarah's child and she might go back to him.

He couldn't bear to think of that happening! Oh, no! Perhaps he was being selfish but he wanted Sarah to stay on here in Rome. He cared deeply for her.

But it was going to be so difficult working with her now that he knew she was pregnant. Pronto Soccorso wasn't an easy department to work in. Maybe he should have her transferred to an easier department. Maybe…maybe he should wait until morning and hope that the situation didn't seem as impossible as it did tonight.

Or perhaps he should phone Sarah to see how she was feeling now. On reflection he felt that his reaction had been a bit harsh when she'd first told him she was pregnant. She needed his support at a time like this, not criticism.

Carlos picked up his mobile before he could change his mind.

CHAPTER FIVE

'SARAH, is that you?'

'Of course it's me.' Sarah felt a rush of happiness as she recognised Carlos's voice.

Carlos hesitated, feeling worried about Sarah being alone with this big problem to sort out. 'Your voice sounded strange, not a bit like you usually sound.'

'Really? Well, I'm the only one in the room, apart from Charlie.'

'Charlie! Who's Charlie?'

'My baby. My gut feeling is that she's a girl, so I'm going to call her Charlotte, Charlie for short and just in case she's a boy. Why have you phoned me, Carlos?'

'I just wanted to make sure you were OK.'

'Of course I'm OK. Just washing out some bits and pieces.'

She wiped her still damp hand on a towel and stretched out on the bed again so that she could enjoy this unexpected conversation. She was feeling much better now that Carlos had dropped his holier-than-thou attitude.

'Sarah, I think you should phone Robin as soon as possible.'

Oh, dear, Carlos was exerting his authority again! Sarah sighed as she listened. She'd thought—or rather hoped—that he'd phoned up for a romantic reason, maybe to invite her round for…

'Sarah, you need to know how Robin's going to react before…well, before you make any plans for the future.'

'Carlos, I'll get in touch with Robin soon. It's not as if

he's desperately waiting for a phone call from me. We did completely split up, you know.'

'I wouldn't say you'd completely split up, otherwise you wouldn't be carrying Robin's child, would you? Call him and then let me know his reaction, will you?'

'You'll be the first person I inform when I've spoken to Robin. Was there anything else?'

She was holding her breath. Anything else as in you've decided you'd like to come round to my room to tell me you love me, that my pregnancy hasn't made the slightest difference to you and—

'I think you should phone Lucy. Your sister will be a tower of strength, won't she?'

'Yes, she will.'

Sarah swallowed hard. She knew that Carlos had suggested she contact Lucy because her twin was the sensible one. Lucy, always on an even keel, never put a foot wrong. A brilliant doctor, a brilliant person. She loved her older-by-ten-minutes sister but sometimes it irked her that she was dismissed as the scatty one.

'I'll phone tomorrow.'

'Good. Well, I'll say goodnight, Sarah. I hope you sleep well.'

'Thank you, I'm sure I will. Goodnight, Carlos.'

She was sure she wouldn't sleep well! All these problems running around in her head. Robin, Lucy. And what about her parents? Her mother would be hopping mad and demand she come straight home. Whereupon she would point out that she was almost thirty years old and could look after herself.

Well, she was going to try not to worry about all that tonight, she told herself as she hung her briefs on the piece of string she'd rigged up in the shower room. Was it in *Gone with the Wind* that somebody had said, 'Tomorrow is another day'? In the same film somebody had also said they didn't give a damn!

She wished she could adopt the same attitude to her present problems!

Her first thought next morning was the phone call to Robin. As soon as she felt wide enough awake, she checked his number in the back of her diary. She also consulted the section of her diary that gave world times and calculated that it should be a reasonable time to call in Robin's part of Africa. Hopefully he would be around.

'Robin? It's Sarah.'

'Sarah! What a surprise!'

She couldn't believe she'd got through almost immediately. When she'd asked to speak to Dr Robin Hardcastle, she'd hadn't expected to be put through so quickly. Almost too quickly! She needed time to compose her thoughts. She'd half hoped he wouldn't be there.

She took a deep breath. 'I thought I might have a problem finding you but—'

'I just happened to be in the office here, checking on some last-minute arrangements with the medical secretary. I've got to go to our clinic upcountry in a few minutes. How are you?'

'I'm... Well, that's what I'm phoning about. Can you talk?'

Robin laughed. 'In French or in English? Why so secretive? What...?'

'Robin...I'm pregnant.'

'Can you repeat that? There's a crackle on the line. I thought you said... Oh, my God, you did, didn't you? You said... Oh, Sarah!'

'Look, I'm only phoning to let you know that you're going to be a father but—'

'Oh, my God! Are you sure?' he lowered his voice. 'And are you sure it's mine?'

'Of course I'm sure it's yours! It was that time you came round before Christmas so—'

'What a terrible thing to happen! Look, I can't talk now—'

'Don't worry, Robin. I'm very happy to be a single mum. I'm only phoning you because I thought you should know. It won't affect my career because I've got a very understanding boss at the Ospedale Tevere. I'll have the baby here in Rome and—'

'Hold on a minute. Don't I get a say in what happens?'

'Only if you want to be involved, Robin. I'll acknowledge you as the father and you can have as much access to the child as you want but—'

'Sarah, you're running ahead of me here! You've had time to digest all this but I'm in a state of shock. I do want to be involved, but at the moment I don't know how much, if you get my meaning. Are you sure you're OK?'

'I'm fine. Look, don't worry about me.'

'I can't help worrying. I wish I was there with you so we could have a proper discussion but I've got to go. I'm going upcountry for a couple of weeks. Communication is difficult up there. As soon as I get back I'll phone you. Take care of yourself, and…well, be careful because…'

The line crackled until it was impossible to distinguish what Robin was saying. Sarah put down the phone and crossed over to the shower room. There, she'd done the dutiful early morning call she'd been planning when she'd lain awake worrying during the night. She'd told Robin he was going to be a father. What kind of a father he chose to be was up to him.

But she hoped against hope he wouldn't get any ideas about forming a family unit, because Robin was the last person in the world she would want to spend her life with.

Unlikely, considering his first reaction had been, 'What a terrible thing to happen!' He'd said he didn't know how much he wanted to be involved. For Charlie's sake it was important she should at least know who her father was. That went without saying.

She reached up and removed her undies from the piece of string. They were still damp so she hung them on the radiator, before taking down the string. The shower room was too tiny for both her and the washing. As the water cascaded over her she reflected that she was feeling fit again, something she didn't usually feel at this time in the morning.

She soaped her abdomen, looking for signs that it might be expanding. Still nice and flat. But not for long! She was quite prepared now. She was going to sail through this pregnancy. She was actually looking forward to being a mother. A single mother. She could cope with whatever life threw at her.

Her first priority on getting to hospital that morning was to see Giacomo because he was going to the theatre for plastic surgery to his legs. After that, she wanted to go along to see Marcellina and give her the results of the tests that she'd just picked up from the lab. Giacomo was understandably apprehensive. Sarah listened carefully as her patient poured out his worries.

'I've never had a general anaesthetic before, Sarah. Never even been in hospital before. Supposing I don't come round from the anaesthetic…not that anybody in the world cares whether I come round or not…'

'I care.'

The words slipped out before she had time to think about the implications. She'd tried so hard to be utterly professional with her patient, but she felt so sorry for him.

Giacomo gave a weak smile. 'Do you, Sarah?'

'We all care, Jack.'

'Absolutely!' Carlos had arrived, coming up behind Sarah, lightly touching her arm before leaning over their patient. 'The surgeon performing your operation is one of the best in Italy. There's nothing to be afraid of, Giacomo.'

'If you say so,' their patient muttered. 'But I wish they'd put bandages over my legs. Why have they left them open all this time?'

'There are many different ways of treating burns,' Carlos explained. 'Mario Pellegrino, our plastic surgeon, believes the open method is the best and he gets excellent results. Once you've had your skin grafts you'll begin to see a big improvement.'

'You'll just have to be patient, I'm afraid,' Sarah put in quietly.

Carlos sat down beside their patient. 'We're spending a lot of time and money to ensure you finish up with the most fantastic new legs. Everybody will be amazed when they hear what you've gone through—especially the girls!'

Giacomo's mouth twitched and then, very slowly, he smiled. 'I never thought of that. I'll be sort of...sort of the bionic man, won't I, Carlos?'

Carlos smiled. 'Something like that. Believe me, you've a lot going for you, Giacomo.'

'Which reminds me,' Sarah said. 'Did you write that letter to Lauren?'

Giacomo grinned. 'It's in my cupboard. Will you post it for me?'

'Of course I will.'

A senior nurse arrived at the bedside. 'Time for your premed, Giacomo.'

'You're in good hands, Jack!' Sarah said as she picked up the letter.

Carlos caught up with Sarah in the corridor. 'What was all that about a letter?'

Sarah smiled. 'Giacomo met an English girl who's working as a waitress. He's written to explain why he missed a date with her.'

'Poor Giacomo!' Carlos said. 'I hope the girl comes to see him. He needs something to cheer him up. Now, where are you hurrying off to?'

'I got the results of Marcellina's tests from the lab. Everything points to the fact that she has a severely underactive thyroid.'

'So your hunch was right.'

'Yes. When I checked up on Marcellina after she'd been admitted I discovered a whole range of symptoms she hadn't mentioned. We knew she was suffering from exhaustion, loss of hair, lower back pain and depression, but also her periods were very irregular, she suffered from panic attacks, her skin was dry and itchy, her toes often felt numb. She was a classic case.'

'Some of those symptoms apply to other medical conditions. Have you—?'

'I've eliminated all the other conditions that display similar symptoms. It's definitely hypothyroidism. I'm referring her to our consultant endocrinologist.'

Carlos nodded. 'Good. Well done, Sarah!'

'Grazie, dottore.'

They were turning the corner that led to the preliminary medical unit. Carlos put his hand on her arm to detain her.

'Wait a moment. We need to talk. First of all, did you sleep well?'

She looked up at him, noting the enigmatic expression on his face, the professional tone of his voice. He was simply being the good doctor, the old family friend, discharging his duties.

'I slept very well, thank you,' she replied in a polite, distant tone.

There was no point elaborating about how she'd tossed and turned, worrying about whether she and Carlos would

Play The Lucky Hearts Game

and get... FREE BOOKS & a FREE GIFT... YOURS to KEEP!

Yes! I have scratched off the silver card. Please send me my **FREE BOOKS** and **FREE MYSTERY GIFT**. I understand that I am under no obligation to purchase any books as explained on the back of this card. I am over 18 years of age.

Scratch Here! then look below to see what you can claim...

M4GI

Mrs/Miss/Ms/Mr _____ Initials _____

BLOCK CAPITALS PLEASE

Surname _____

Address _____

_____

Postcode _____

Twenty-one gets you **4 FREE BOOKS** and a **MYSTERY GIFT!**

Twenty gets you **1 FREE BOOK** and a **MYSTERY GIFT!**

Nineteen gets you **1 FREE BOOK!**

TRY AGAIN!

The Reader Service™ — Here's how it works:

THE READER SERVICE™
FREE BOOK OFFER
FREEPOST CN81
CROYDON
CR9 3WZ

NO STAMP
NECESSARY
IF POSTED IN
THE U.K. OR N.I.

ever get together again. He was making it obvious he'd lost all interest in her as a desirable woman.

'And have you made any phone calls yet?'

'I've phoned Robin.'

'You have? And what did he say when you told him…the news?'

'He said, and I quote, "What a terrible thing to happen."'

Carlos's eyes clouded over. 'Were you upset when he said that?'

'Well, I wasn't overjoyed by his reaction, but it was certainly predictable. I told you that Robin wouldn't want to be a father, well, not in the accepted sense of the word.'

'What do you mean?'

'Robin indicated that he wanted to be involved with his child, but he didn't know how much.'

Carlos frowned. 'I don't understand.'

'Neither do I! But it was a complete shock to him. He hasn't had time to think it through. Knowing Robin, I think what he means is that he'd like to see his child occasionally, send cards and presents when appropriate but maintain his independence from family life. Something like that! But I'm merely guessing.'

'Are you sure that's the kind of father he will be? After the baby's born, don't you think he'll want to become more involved? He might even want to form a family unit. Fatherhood does strange things to the most unpaternal of men.'

Sarah sighed. 'Carlos, I can't be sure of anything at the moment,' she said, in an exasperated tone. 'The line was crackly, there were people listening in to what Robin was saying. He's going to call me back in a couple of weeks so that we can discuss the situation in more detail.'

'I can't see how any man could ignore his child like that!

I'm sure he'll want to play a major role in his child's life. As I told you, once the baby is born—'

'Carlos, this is my problem and I'll sort it out my way. So, if you don't mind, I'm going to go and see Marcellina and explain about her hypothyroidism.'

'Don't spend too long. I've made an appointment for you to see Alessandro Prassede this morning.'

She turned round, her hand on the swing door of the medical unit. 'You mean the obstetric consultant?'

'Well, that's the kind of doctor that pregnant women consult, isn't it? There's nothing strange in—'

'Carlos, you had no right to make this appointment! How dare you be so high-handed?'

A nurse pushed through the swing doors from the other side. Sarah removed her hand and stood looking up Carlos, her eyes flashing dangerously.

For a moment she saw the hint of a smile on Carlos's lips and that infuriated her even more.

'This is my baby and—'

She lowered her voice as she saw the nurse glancing back at this interesting encounter between the medical director of Pronto Soccorso and the new English doctor.

'The appointment is at eleven,' Carlos said evenly. 'I'll escort you there and introduce you, if you like.'

'To make sure I don't cancel? I might prefer to go to another hospital for my antenatal care.'

Carlos raised one eyebrow. 'Indeed you might, but if you're to fulfil your contractual obligations to the Ospedale Tevere, it's better that you don't have to spend time too much time travelling to and from another hospital.'

'Now you're pulling rank on me.' She paused to review the situation. 'But I suppose you're right.'

Carlos put his hands on either side of her shoulders and held them there for a few moments. She remained absolutely still.

'You may find me infuriating,' he said quietly, 'but I only have your best interests at heart. I want you to have the best antenatal care possible. I've known Alessandro Prassede a long time. He's one of the best obstetricians in Rome. When I phoned him earlier this morning, he told me he'd just had a cancellation, otherwise you would have had to go on his waiting list and the baby might have been born by the time he could see you.'

Sarah couldn't help smiling. Carlos always liked to have the last word in an argument, but she had to admit that this obstetrician sounded excellent. And she'd decided that she wanted nothing but the best for her daughter.

'Thank you, Carlos. I'm really very grateful. Now, if you'll excuse me…'

As she turned away from him and went into the medical unit she felt a moment of panic. She'd always liked to be in control, but her hold on her own lifestyle was being taken away from her. Everything was changing and she knew it was only going to become more complicated as the weeks passed.

So she really should be grateful for the interest Carlos was taking in her. He was being totally professional and detached. She groaned inwardly as she thought of the romantic rapport that had existed between them yesterday. That would never return. Not now that Carlos simply viewed her as an old friend and a medical colleague requiring extra care and attention.

She gave herself a mental shake. Thank goodness for her work! Work always focussed her mind and made her see how unimportant her own problems were compared with the trauma of her patients.

She forced a smile on to her face as she approached Marcellina's bed. Her patient was sitting in an armchair, reading.

'Marcellina, I've got your test results.'

Marcellina put down her book. 'What's wrong with me?'

'Your thyroid isn't being as efficient as it should be, but we can do something about it.'

'How?'

'One pill a day. It's that simple.'

'Really?' Marcellina smiled. 'What kind of pill?'

'It's a tiny tablet that contains the hormone thyroxine. You'll be seen by our consultant endocrinologist today and then you'll start the treatment. As soon as the thyroxine starts working and you feel stronger, you'll be able to go home and lead a normal life.'

'But that's wonderful!'

Sarah stayed for a few minutes, answering Marcellina's questions about the treatment she was going to receive. When she came away, she was feeling happier than when she'd gone in. It was good to help a patient to stop worrying.

Worrying was futile. She was going to be as positive as she could be during the months ahead.

Back in Pronto Soccorso, she treated a little boy with a long gash in his right arm. He'd been climbing over some railings when he'd caught it on one of the spikes. His anxious mother watched as Sarah finished suturing the wound.

'I'm not going to let Matteo play outside the garden again,' she said fiercely.

'Oh, Mamma!' the boy remonstrated, lifting up his arm to show that he was OK. 'I'm six years old. My friends will think I'm a baby if you don't let me go out to play.'

'I think Matteo's right,' Sarah said carefully. 'In England we always say that boys will be boys. I'm sure it's the same here in Italy. Sometimes he will get hurt but that's life, isn't it? And this wound will soon heal. Bring him back next week and I'll take out the stitches.'

'Thank you, *Dottore*. You've been very kind. Do you have any children of your own?' she went on.

Sarah hesitated. For a moment she was almost tempted to confide in this motherly lady. But the moment passed as her professional self got the better of her.

'No, I haven't any children,' Sarah said. 'Why do you ask?'

'You seemed to have such a natural manner with my little Matteo. You're still young, *Dottore*, but don't leave it too long before you have children of your own. My children are the most important part of my life. I have two small daughters younger than Matteo.' She leaned forward to whisper, 'And I've just found out I'm going to have another baby at the end of the summer.'

Sarah drew in her breath. 'Congratulations!'

'*Dottore!*' Maria was standing at the door of the cubicle, looking agitated. 'Can you help me with a patient?'

'Of course!' Sarah smiled at Matteo and his mother. 'Goodbye. See you next week.'

Sarah took over from Maria with a difficult patient who was complaining of a pain in the chest. He said he wanted to be seen at once and claimed to have been waiting too long to see a doctor.

Sarah fixed her stethoscope in her ears. She could find nothing wrong with his heart, but she wired him up to a monitor to find out what was going on. Several tests later she was able to advise the patient that his heart was perfectly sound and healthy.

At that moment, the patient gave a loud burp. 'There! That's better. Pain's gone now, *Dottore*,' he said as he climbed off the examination couch. '*Ciao!*'

'Just a moment!'

Sarah put out her hand to detain him but the patient went out through the cubicle door, almost colliding with Carlos who was on his way in.

'Well, of all the time-wasting…!' Sarah began, placing her hands on her hips.

Carlos smiled. 'What was the problem?'

'There was absolutely nothing wrong with that man. That sometimes happened to me in London and it's infuriating!'

Carlos touched her arm gently. 'Sarah! You mustn't worry about it. You've got an important consultation with Alessandro Prassede in a few minutes and he won't want you to arrive in an agitated state. Besides it's not good for the baby.'

Sarah looked down at her abdomen. 'Poor little Charlie! Having a working mum like me. She'd have been much better off with a nice maternal type like young Matteo's mum. She was warm, cuddly—'

'Oh, you can work on the cuddly bit when you start putting on weight,' Carlos said with a wry smile.

'Don't remind me about the weight I'll have to carry around!'

'I think it will suit you.'

Carlos's eyes lingered on Sarah's face, before moving downwards to imagine her with luscious full breasts and a more rounded body. She was going to look even more beautiful in the weeks to come. It was going to be so difficult to stifle his desire for her!

'*Andiamo!* Let's go!' he said quickly. 'I'll take you to Alessandro's consulting rooms but I'll probably be called back before long.'

'You really don't need to come with me. I—'

'Oh, but I want to come. What are friends for?'

As she fell into step beside Carlos, Sarah knew she would have to come to terms with the fact that Carlos had no interest in her as a desirable woman. What man could possibly consider loving a woman who was carrying another man's child?

She must resign herself to the inevitable and get rid of

her stupid romantic yearnings. Their romance was over—well, for the foreseeable future. She wasn't going to relinquish all hope of seducing Carlos after Charlie was born and she'd got her figure back.

They were passing the door to the obstetrics ward. The sound of a newborn baby crying made her stop absolutely still. In a few months' time she would be in there, holding little Charlie in her arms.

She fished in her pocket for a tissue as she turned back to look at Carlos. Hastily dabbing her eyes, she said, 'Come on, Carlos. Don't want to be late.'

Carlos reached forward and took the tissue from her hand. 'You've missed a bit,' he said as he gently wiped her damp cheek. 'Do you always cry in sympathy with the babies?'

She sniffed. 'Not usually. I can deliver other people's babies without it affecting me emotionally, but hearing that baby crying just now…'

Carlos put out his arms and drew her against him. 'You're going to be fine, Sarah. You're a brave girl and—Oh, *buongiorno*, Alessandro!'

Sarah had been enjoying the feel of Carlos's arms around her but she sprang quickly away from him as the distinguished consultant stood in front of them.

'*Buongiorno*, Carlos.' The consultant switched to heavily accented but perfectly grammatical English. 'You must be Dr Montgomery from England. Do come this way.'

Sarah took an immediate liking to the man who was going to care for her throughout her pregnancy. He hadn't looked the slightest bit puzzled by the fact that she and Carlos had seemed to be locked in an embrace outside the obstetrics ward.

A thought occurred to her. Perhaps Alessandro Prassede thought Carlos was the father of her baby. But Carlos would have told him that Sarah was just an old friend who'd been working in London. Still, that didn't prove anything. She and Carlos, although good friends, might possibly have been lovers.

They would most certainly have been lovers yesterday if she hadn't dropped her bombshell.

'Do come in, Sarah. May I call you Sarah?'

'Of course, er…'

'Please, call me Alessandro. Now, do sit down next to Carlos here.'

Sarah found the informality of Alessandro's consulting room was very relaxing. She was seated next to Carlos on a comfortable sofa. Alessandro was seated to one side of them in an easy chair. There was a notepad and pen on the small coffee-table beside him.

Sarah wondered how long Carlos was going to stay. Having discharged his duties as good friend and senior colleague, she would have thought he would want to hurry back to Pronto Soccorso.

She could tell that Alessandro was trying to gain her confidence as he chatted in English about the cold weather in Rome at the moment. Was it colder than this in London? How awful! He'd spent a whole winter in England working in a hospital when he was a junior doctor and he'd been so happy to return to Rome. He couldn't wait for the spring weather to arrive when he and his family could live outdoors at the weekends.

'So, when do you think your baby is due, Sarah? I expect you've worked that one out?'

'Of course. The first day of my last period was the fifth of December so if we add seven days and nine calendar months that comes out at the twelfth of September, making a total of forty weeks. Of course that's only approximate and may vary by ten days either way so it's important that—'

She broke off in embarrassment. She'd cared for so many pregnant women who'd needed the full explanation that for a moment she'd forgotten she was talking to a consultant obstetrician.

Alessandro smiled. 'You're used to spelling it out to your patients, aren't you, Sarah?' He hesitated. 'It's quite different when you're the patient, isn't it?'

Sarah smiled back at the charming man. She felt utterly reassured by his calm manner.

'It's certainly going to be a challenge. Oh, don't get me wrong, I'm looking forward to being a mother but it's certainly going to change my life.'

'Yes, my wife and I have got five children. We planned four, but the fourth pregnancy was twins so…'

'I'm a twin!'

'How interesting! Would you like to have twins yourself?'

'I'd prefer one baby to start with. I'm a complete novice as a mum!'

Alessandro laughed. 'All my first time patients say that but they soon get the hang of it. It's all perfectly natural.'

Sarah looked across at Carlos. He'd been listening to their exchange but hadn't spoken. He was simply there for moral support. She began to feel that the strong support she had in this hospital was going to carry her through. There was no need to be apprehensive any more.

'So how long do you plan to work, Sarah?' Alessandro had picked up his notepad.

'I was thinking—'

Carlos leaned forward and put a hand on Sarah's arm. 'As you know, Alessandro, Sarah is working in Pronto Soccorso. I've advised her to begin her maternity leave when she's thirty-two weeks pregnant in July. The strenuous work required in the department is dangerous for a pregnant doctor so it's not advisable to stay any longer.'

Alessandro nodded. 'Are you happy with that, Sarah?'

She looked at Carlos and knew she had to trust his judgement. If this was what Carlos recommended, that's what she would do.

Sarah nodded. 'Absolutely. Carlos has been giving me excellent advice.'

For a moment Alessandro looked perplexed. 'Yes, but Carlos has a vested interest in taking good care of...of his staff.'

Sarah was beginning to get the picture. Alessandro definitely thought she was involved with Carlos and that he was possibly the father of her child. Man of the world as he obviously was, Alessandro wasn't asking any direct questions about who the father was. He was simply concerned with caring for her during her pregnancy. The question of who had fathered her child was unimportant.

How refreshing! She smiled as she looked across at her new consultant obstetrician, waiting for him to explain what else he needed to know before, presumably, he examined her.

Alessandro put down his notebook after making a few brief notes. Sarah noticed him press a bell at the side of his desk. A white-uniformed nurse came in, looking enquiringly at her boss.

'Would you take Sarah and prepare her for an antenatal examination? I'll be along in a few minutes.'

'Of course.'

Carlos stood up. Sarah hoped he wasn't going to accompany her to the next part of the proceedings. She'd been happy to have him with her in the consulting room but during an obstetric examination was out of the question.

'I must return to Pronto Soccorso, Alessandro,' Carlos said.

The two consultants shook hands.

Carlos turned to Sarah. 'I'll phone you later.'

'I'll be back in the department before—'

Carlos shook his head. 'I really think you should take the rest of the day off. We're well staffed and you'll need to rest after your examination and all the tests Alessandro will put you through.'

Carlos smiled at his colleague before leaving.

Sarah lay on her bed, staring at the ceiling. Yes, Carlos had been right, she did need a rest after her examination. Alessandro had been nothing if not thorough. Specimens of blood had been taken for grouping, the rhesus factor and haemoglobin estimation. Wasserman Kahn tests had been carried out to exclude syphilis. Her urine had been tested for protein, glucose and ketoacids.

She'd had a full cardiovascular examination and had had her blood pressure taken several times. A vaginal examination had followed and then she'd undergone an ultrasound scan. It had been exciting to see the tiny pinprick of light flashing which indicated that her baby's heart was beating.

One baby only, not twins. Unless another baby was hidden behind its twin. But unless later scans proved otherwise, she would consider herself to be carrying a single foetus.

That had been the most poignant moment of the whole morning. After that she'd felt so emotionally moved that she'd been relieved that Carlos had given her the rest of the day off.

She decided that it must be all these hormonal changes that were making her weepy but her eyes had seemed continually moist ever since she'd seen that tiny flashing light.

She patted her abdomen. 'Keep going, Charlie, we're going to make it, you and me. No problem.'

She leaned across the bed and picked up her mobile.

Now to give Lucy the startling news that she was pregnant. With any luck she'd catch her sister on her lunch-break.

'Lucy!'

'Sarah, what a lovely surprise. I was just thinking about you.'

'Well, twins are supposed to be telepathic, aren't they?'

'We've never found that before, have we?'

'Absolutely not,' Sarah said, 'otherwise you would have known my news before I got around to telling you.'

Lucy laughed. 'Go on, give me a clue and then I can claim I'm psychic. You're not pregnant, are you?'

Sarah gasped. 'Got it in one!'

'I don't believe it!'

'Why did you think I was pregnant?'

'I didn't. It was about the most unlikely thing that could happen to you. I mean, I know you were living with Robin but you've never wanted kids, have you? Anyway, I thought you'd split up before you went to Rome.'

'We did split up...but we had one last fling, sort of for old times' sake, wasn't it fun while it lasted, kind of thing. And it was helped along by some pre-Christmas champagne.'

'So, what do you want me to say, Sarah? Congratulations or what are you going to do about this unplanned pregnancy?'

Sarah took a deep breath. Ever the practical one, her twin!

'I don't mind what you say, Lucy. I'm planning to have my baby as a single mum and—'

'Good for you, Sarah! I presume you'll be taking maternity leave?'

'Three months, mid-July to mid-October. My baby's due in September. Carlos thought I shouldn't work in A and E after I was thirty-two weeks.'

'Carlos is quite right. How is he?'

'Fine! He's been very supportive.'

'Good.' Lucy paused. 'Do you think Carlos would like me to take over from you while you're on maternity leave? You'll need a replacement, won't you?'

Sarah felt a rush of relief. It would be great to have her sister around when her baby was due.

'Lucy, that would be wonderful! I'd love to have you around when I'm in the final weeks. It would certainly help to solve Carlos's staffing problems. And as you've got exactly the same medical qualifications as me and you've had similar experience in A and E, the medical board would be sure to approve Carlos's recommendation.'

'Sarah, do you think Carlos would approve of the idea?'

'I'm sure he'll be delighted that we've saved him the problem of finding a good doctor for three months. And we're so much alike that the rest of the staff will probably not notice I've gone! But what about your own job?'

Another pause. 'I'd welcome a break, Sarah. I'll put in for three months' leave of absence. When the hospital board hears that I'm going to gain further experience of accident and emergency techniques by working in a state-of-the-art Italian hospital, there'll be no problem.'

Sarah hesitated. Her sister had always been the secretive one. It had been obvious for some time to Sarah that Lucy was having a difficult time. But even though they were so close, she hadn't wanted to pry. Lucy had never wanted anyone to pity her. Sarah knew that she mustn't ask questions. She would be told in due course if there was anything she should know, or if she could help in any way.

'Lucy, I'll speak to Carlos tomorrow and get back to you. Thanks ever so much. I feel really relieved that you're coming out here.'

'To be honest, it's just what I need. I've been…well, I need a break.'

Sarah waited a few seconds, hoping that Lucy might elaborate, but there was no more information forthcoming.

'I'll get back to you as soon as I can, Lucy. Bye…'

CHAPTER SIX

LOOKING out of the window of her small office, Sarah felt a welcome lifting of her spirits. It was the beginning of April and spring was definitely lurking just around the corner somewhere. The trees at the edge of the hospital forecourt were covered in leaves whereas when she'd first arrived they'd looked very bare and bleak in the early morning.

The weeks were passing by so quickly. Too quickly! This was her last spring as an independent person. At the end of the summer she would have another little person to care for and life would never be the same again.

She leaned back in her chair as she pushed the medical case notes she'd been checking to one side. She was glad that Carlos had assigned her this tiny room off the corridor that led to Pronto Soccorso. At the beginning of each working day she'd started sorting out her paperwork in here. And if there was a rare quiet moment during the day she popped in here to put her feet up. She was only four months pregnant but she knew the importance of relaxing whenever she could.

She was also grateful that Carlos had made it clear he wasn't going to consider her for night duty. Sometimes, when she crawled into her bed at the end of a long day, she was absolutely whacked. She needed her sleep more than she'd ever done. Trying to sleep during the day after a long shift on night duty had never been her strong point. But now her body sometimes cried out for rest at the end of the day.

And she had another five months to go! Carlos had asked

her if she would like to work part time. She'd insisted that wasn't an option. Having been at the hospital such a short time, she didn't want to be sidelined at this stage. As long as she got a good night's sleep, she could cope perfectly well.

Yes, Carlos had been very supportive since she'd told him she was pregnant. He'd readily agreed to the idea that Lucy should come out to Rome to take over from her during her three months' maternity leave and he'd told her that the medical board had approved the arrangement.

Alessandro had been pleased with Sarah's progress when she'd gone to see him yesterday for another antenatal examination. The ultrasound had confirmed there was single foetus. She knew she couldn't wish for better support than she was receiving during her pregnancy, so why did she continually have this feeling of longing for something more?

As her pregnancy had progressed she'd been surprised how her longing for a strong, physical, sexual relationship with Carlos had increased. Her sexual appetite was undiminished by the changes in her growing body. For a few days, immediately after she'd told Carlos she was pregnant, he'd seemed wary of making any physical advances towards her. But whenever he'd leaned towards her for an affectionate kiss she'd made sure that she'd signalled her need for something more.

At first she'd sensed that Carlos was trying to come to terms with the fact that she was carrying another man's child. Sometimes he seemed to be holding himself in check, trying to stifle his desires. But she sensed that his desires, like her own, were growing stronger each time they were alone together. The fact that Carlos seemed to still find her desirable was wonderful, and so unexpected!

She sighed as she reflected on the tenderness of his caresses. As the weeks passed, she longed for the times when he held her in his arms, caressed her, told her that her pregnancy was making her even more beautiful. And when he kissed her, she clung to him, longing for total fulfilment of her love for him.

But he always held back from the ultimate consummation and she remained frustrated. She'd seen the beads of sweat on Carlos's skin as he'd pulled away from her before they'd reached the point of no return. She knew that the frustration was difficult for her to bear but for Carlos, hot-blooded, passionate Carlos, it must be ten times worse!

She groaned out loud as she allowed herself to reflect on what might have been if Carlos had still regarded her as a free woman. For a brief moment she allowed herself to dwell on that day in his parents' apartment. At the end of their wonderful day together Carlos had been her soul-mate, waiting to consummate their love, and she'd wanted him so much…

She took a deep breath until she felt she had her emotions under control again. Even now, she could feel her heart beating more quickly as she remembered how desperately she'd wanted to make love with Carlos. It had been completely heartbreaking to have to break off and tell him the devastating truth just as they'd been…

'I thought I'd find you here, Sarah.'

Carlos was standing in the doorway.

'I did knock but there's so much noise going on out here in the corridor that—Are you all right?'

He was at the side of her desk now, looking down at her with concerned eyes. As he drew her against him, she raised her face, her lips parting with anticipation. His kiss was brief but tender.

She could feel her cheeks becoming flushed. She hadn't expected Carlos to walk in on her when she was having such lustful thoughts about him. She always tried to keep her sensual emotions under control when she was in hospital.

He frowned. 'You look hot, Sarah. What's the matter?' He pressed his hand against her forehead. 'No, you're OK now. Do you often get flushed like this?'

She shook her head. 'No, no, I was surprised to see you, that's all. How was your weekend with your parents?'

He raised his eyebrows. 'Too many problems at the Villa Florissa, the one you used to stay in.'

'What sort of problems?'

'Oh, the plumbers are installing new bathrooms and my mother changed her mind about the décor last week. The plumbers walked out and I had to go down and negotiate for their return. Then I had to persuade my mother that the new décor she'd originally chosen was an excellent choice.'

Sarah smiled. She would have loved a couple of days down on the coast in the house where she'd spent her summers as a child. After all, that had been where she'd first met Carlos. If only he'd asked her to go with him! Just to revive the happy memories.

'The house is going to look great when it's finished. My parents send you their regards.'

'Did you tell them about…?'

'I told them you were working here. I didn't tell them you were pregnant.'

Sarah pulled a wry face. 'No, of course you didn't. Your mother wouldn't approve, would she?'

Carlos shrugged his shoulders. 'Probably not.'

He looked down at Sarah, holding back the desire to take her in his arms again. Sometimes it was sheer torture when he was near her to quell his desires. During that brief period when she'd first arrived here in Rome and he'd found himself falling in love with her he'd been unable to believe what had been happening. But finding out that she was pregnant, that she was carrying another man's child, had been such a shock.

He'd known he had to support Sarah whatever happened. But the rights of the father of her child and his own sense of family values were conflicting. It had been so difficult to hold back his emotions. Impossible to stop himself wanting to make love with Sarah.

But did he have the right to think about her as a desirable woman when it was Robin who should be here with her during her pregnancy? And he couldn't discount the idea that Robin might arrive here one day and ask Sarah to be his wife. Robin might take Sarah and the unborn child away with him and it would be unforgivable of him to try to intervene between a father and his family.

If only Sarah were his wife and the child she was carrying were his! She would seem even more desirable to him—if that were possible! He would be able to make love to her without the constant feeling of guilt that came to him. Whenever he took her in his arms now, the spectre of that other man cast its shadow.

Would it make a difference if he could be absolutely sure that Robin had relinquished all interest in the child she was carrying?

It might.

He took a deep breath as he sat down on a chair at the side of Sarah's desk and asked if she'd heard from Robin again.

Sarah frowned. 'He phoned again last night. He's still undecided about how much involvement he wants.'

Carlos put the heel of his hand against his forehead. '*Mamma mia!* How much longer does that man think you're going to wait? Why can't he give you a straight answer? Didn't he have anything different to say this time?'

Sarah cleared her throat nervously. Carlos would hit the roof when he heard Robin's latest idea!

'Robin is thinking he might come to Rome for a couple of weeks. He's not sure if he—'

Carlos leapt to his feet. 'He might come! He's not sure! Everything is so…so indecisive about this man! Why can't he make up his mind? What is so difficult about making a decision?'

'Robin hates making decisions. Every time he's phoned me he's simply been sounding me out. Asking me what he thinks we should do and—'

'*We* should do? So he really is now considering you and the baby as part of his family?'

She hesitated. 'I get the impression he's putting forward the dutiful ideas for me to consider. I give him the same answers every time. I don't want a dutiful partnership with him.'

Carlos walked across the room and stared unseeingly out of the window. What would he do if this man came to Rome and persuaded Sarah to go away with him? In terms of family values, the man had more rights over Sarah and the baby than he had.

He swung round. 'Did Robin say when he might come to Rome?'

Sarah walked towards Carlos putting up one hand to smooth away the lines on his furrowed brow.

'No, he didn't. It's just one of his nebulous ideas. I think he only said it because it sounded like the dutiful thing to do. I told him we could discuss everything that needs to be said over the phone and—'

'Oh, Sarah!' Carlos drew her into his arms, his lips seeking hers for the reassurance he needed.

A moment later he was pulling himself away, taking deep breaths to regain his composure. Here in hospital wasn't the place for him to contemplate how madly jealous and worried he was about the impossible situation. But he couldn't wait any longer for Robin to make up his mind.

From what Sarah had told him, the man seemed completely unreliable. He didn't deserve Sarah or his unborn child!

Carlos frowned as he thought about what action he should take. By refusing to make important decisions that affected Sarah and her unborn child, Robin was surely indicating that he wanted minimum involvement. That was Sarah's interpretation and she knew the man better than he did.

He'd been very patient, but wouldn't he now be justified in moving his relationship with Sarah one step further? The way she clung to him, moulded her wonderful body against his whenever he held her in his arms told him Sarah was longing for consummation as much as he was.

Standing so close to her now, he felt a frisson of excitement running through him. Sarah, more beautiful than ever with her swelling breasts and voluptuous curves, had the instant power to arouse him. He'd found her so utterly desirable since those heady days soon after she'd arrived here in Rome. Every day he'd longed to hold her in his arms. During the time they'd spent a whole day together seeing the sights in Rome, he'd had to hold himself in check.

He remembered that fateful day now, the actual moment when they'd been standing in the middle of the temple of Jupiter and he'd planned to make love to Sarah that evening…to hold her in his arms.

She'd been wearing the same perfume she was wearing today. It had heightened his senses as it was doing at the moment. He'd been so sure that Sarah had wanted him as much as he'd wanted her.

But he'd been blissfully unaware that she was pregnant until—

'Carlos, I really must go and do some work.'

'Sarah, will you spend this evening with me?'

'I'd love to!'

She couldn't disguise her excitement. She always looked

forward to spending a whole evening with Carlos. Sometimes they went to a concert or a theatre. Often they simply spent the entire evening having dinner in a candlelit restaurant. But going out with Carlos always felt like a special occasion.

It was only at the end of the evening where she had to hold herself in check. She had to try not to lose her sense of reality when Carlos took her in his arms to say goodnight. She had to remember the frustration she would feel if she allowed herself to give in completely to her deep desires. If Carlos could control his sensual emotions, so must she!

Carlos smiled. 'Good! I'll contact you later in the day with more details.'

He leaned forward and put his finger under her chin, tilting her face so that she was looking up at him with those beautiful blue eyes. She had exquisite features. He adored her and always would, whatever happened in the future.

He lowered his head and kissed her gently on her soft, lusciously sensual lips.

Sarah put out her arms and for a brief moment clung to him. Her eyes had closed automatically as she'd savoured his kiss. She was trying so hard not to allow her body to react but the desire that sprang up inside her was difficult to conceal. She checked the sigh that sprang to her lips as she dragged herself away.

Opening her eyes, she saw that Carlos was regarding her with a strange, enigmatic expression. Maybe she should have held onto her feelings more…but it had been Carlos who had made the first move.

The easiest way out was to leave her room before she became more involved.

'Sarah?'

She turned at the door.

'Could you spare a few minutes to come with me to see Giacomo, our burns patient?' Carlos said, completely professional again. 'I saw him earlier this morning and he asked if you would go along to see him again.'

Sarah frowned. 'But I saw Giacomo only yesterday. His burns are finally healing and I told him he'll be going home at the weekend.'

Carlos shrugged. 'He wants to see you about something important. He was very mysterious when I was there. I'll come along with you. There's another patient in the burns unit I have to see at the same time.'

Carlos allowed himself to put his hand in the small of Sarah's back as they went out into the corridor.

He could tell she'd put on some weight around the middle. It suited her because she'd been too thin.

'So what did Alessandro say when you saw him yesterday?' Carlos asked as they walked along the corridor.

'That I'm in excellent health. My weight is what it should be and…oh, yes…he asked me if I wanted to know the sex of my baby.'

'And?'

Sarah smiled. 'It's a girl. I had a hunch it might be. Well, I had a fifty-fifty chance of getting it right, didn't I? I think I told you I've been calling her Charlie. I'll carry on. I can have her christened Charlotte but she'll always be just Charlie to me.'

'Won't Robin want a say in her name?'

'I don't know. We haven't got around to discussing that.'

She quickened her pace. Carlos seemed obsessed with what Robin thought about her pregnancy. But, then, he didn't know Robin as well as she did.

Or thought she did!

She felt a moment of apprehension. Supposing Robin should suddenly want to have more influence in Charlie's life than she would like? No, no, that wasn't going to happen. But if it did, she would cross that bridge when she came to it.

Carlos met up with Mario Pellegrino, the consultant plastic surgeon, at the entrance to the burns unit. They were deep in discussion as they went to examine a patient who had been transferred from Pronto Soccorso the day before.

Sarah went across to speak to Giacomo. He was sitting in a chair at the side of his bed. His face broke out into a wreath of smiles when he saw her approaching. He stretched out his legs in front of him to show off the healing scars from his burns. After weeks of inactivity he was glad to be able to walk around on crutches for a limited time each day.

'Your legs are healing beautifully, Jack,' Sarah said as she knelt down to make a more detailed examination.

Carefully, she straightened up and moved away from her patient. 'Carlos says you were asking to see me.'

Giacomo smiled broadly. 'You know the girlfriend I told you about?' he said, in English. 'You posted my letter to her, didn't you?'

'Have you had a reply?'

'Better than that! She came to see me last night. I'd had a couple of letters from her saying she'd try to come and see me. I'd actually given up hope but then she just walked in.'

'That's wonderful, Jack!' Sarah said enthusiastically.

'She's coming again this afternoon.'

'I'm so pleased for you.'

'Sarah, there's an emergency. We've got to go!' Carlos arrived at the bedside.

'Three emergency patients all arrived at once,' Carlos told Sarah as they hurried into Pronto Soccorso. 'You take care of this child here. I'll deal with the car crash victims—a young couple. Man driving, badly injured. Heavily pregnant woman. Obstetrics has been alerted…'

Sarah leaned over the two-year-old girl on the examination couch. It was obvious that the toddler was having problems with her breathing. The flesh around her eyes was swollen and she was finding it impossible to open them.

'Can you open your mouth for me, Francesca?' Sarah asked gently.

The child continued wheezing and coughing but as soon as she opened her mouth Sarah was able to confirm her initial diagnosis. Anaphylactic shock.

'Adrenalin, please, Nurse.'

Sarah checked the syringe and made a swift injection. There wasn't a moment to lose. The child's throat was almost closed. She knew that if she'd left her patient's airway untreated for another few minutes it would have been completely blocked by the rapidly swelling tissues. She would have had to perform an emergency tracheostomy.

'Do you know what Francesca is allergic to?' she asked the anxious mother, who was hovering closely.

'She's allergic to peanuts. We're always careful not to have any in the house. But my eldest daughter had some friends round. One of them arrived chewing peanuts. She picked up Francesca and cuddled her before anybody had seen what was happening. My elder daughter could see her friend was chewing something but she didn't know what it was. I was working in the kitchen. I didn't know anything was wrong until Francesca started crying and my eldest daughter brought her in to see me.'

Sarah nodded. 'That's what caused it. Francesca's allergy is so severe that she can be affected if she goes anywhere near peanuts.'

The mother leaned down to give her little daughter a kiss on her forehead. 'Oh, look, the swelling's going down on her eyelids, Doctor!'

'Yes, the injection of adrenalin I gave Francesca is beginning to work. Open your mouth for me, Francesca. There's a good girl.'

Sarah could see that the swelling was already subsiding. She smiled as she patted the little girl's hand.

'Well done! You're going to be fine, Francesca.'

'*Dottore!*' A senior midwife came into the cubicle. 'I need help with my patient...pronto!'

Quickly Sarah assigned the nurse who'd been helping her with Francesca to stay and observe her patient until she returned.

The obstetrics patient in the next cubicle was panting hard as she breathed into an entonox machine. This was obviously the heavily pregnant woman involved in a car crash.

'Violetta has gone into labour but the umbilical cord is too low down,' the midwife told Sarah quietly.

Pulling on sterile gloves, Sarah made a quick assessment. A prolapsed umbilical cord was visible at the head of the birth canal, with the baby's head close behind it. Carefully, she inserted her hand and held it against the baby's head. This prevented the head from pushing against the cord and cutting off the oxygen supply.

She glanced up at the midwife. 'Alert the theatre and the obstetrics team that we're on our way.'

Raising her voice, Sarah called, 'I need a porter to take an emergency patient to Theatre, pronto!'

From a nearby cubicle, Carlos heard Sarah calling for help. Racing inside, he began to push the trolley out of the cubicle in the direction of the corridor that led to the theatre.

A porter arrived close behind him and took over. Carlos took charge of the entonox machine, ensuring that there was a continuous supply of gas and air for their patient as they hurried down the corridor.

'She needs an emergency Caesarean,' Sarah said. 'The baby's head is in danger of pressing against the umbilical cord. I'm trying to hold back the head so that the baby's oxygen supply isn't cut off.'

Sarah was leaning over her patient. As they moved along towards Theatre she kept her hand inside the distended birth canal, pushing the baby's head back so that it couldn't compress the umbilical cord. On the other side of the trolley, Carlos was clutching their patient's hand, comforting her with soothing words as he manipulated the entonox machine, holding the mask over Violetta's face to give her some much-needed pain relief.

The doors of the operating theatre were swung open by one of the obstetrics team.

'Keep panting, Violetta,' Carlos urged their patient. 'You mustn't push.'

The anaesthetist placed a mask over Violetta's face. One of the obstetrics doctors came forward to take over from Sarah.

'You've got to keep the baby's head from pressing against the umbilical cord,' Sarah stressed. 'Look, put your hand right here…OK?'

'OK. You can leave Violetta with us now.'

Sarah checked that the young doctor knew exactly what he was doing. Satisfied, she straightened up and headed for the door. Violetta was blissfully unconscious now. The obstetrics consultant would soon be lifting out a healthy baby from the womb…Sarah hoped.

'Stop worrying,' the young doctor called after Sarah as she pushed open the swing doors. 'I've delivered a few babies in my time, Doctor. I know the dangers of this case.'

Sarah turned round to look at the young man who'd taken over from her. 'Give me a call in Pronto Soccorso to let me know the outcome,' she said quickly.

Carlos was already hurrying back to Pronto Soccorso.

Sarah caught up with him at the entrance as he paused to brief one of the nurses.

'I had to leave a nurse in charge of my car-crash victim when I heard you call out,' he told Sarah. 'Frederico doesn't know his wife has gone into labour.'

'She's not due for another six weeks,' Sarah said, some anxiety creeping into her voice. 'Thanks for coming to my rescue.'

'If it hadn't been me it would have been one of the other doctors I've drafted in from the preliminary units. I just happened to be nearest.'

'Thank goodness!'

Carlos took hold of her hand and lifted it to his lips. She felt a tremor of excitement. Tonight they would spend the whole evening together. But she had to get back to work and stay focussed on her patients now.

'Must go. I've left a nurse to take care of my anaphylactic shock case. She's stabilised now,' Sarah said. 'What injuries has your patient sustained?'

'Fractured femur, midshaft and head. The head of the femur is badly smashed and the upper leg is badly mangled. I'm not sure if the leg is viable or not. The orthopaedic consultant is on his way to assess the situation.'

'You mean Frederico may need an amputation?'

Carlos drew in his breath. 'It's a possibility. I'm not going to tell him his wife is in Theatre until I've stabilised his condition.'

'I've asked the obstetrics team to keep me informed about Violetta,' Sarah said as she began to walk away.

'So have I. We'll compare notes later and decide what we should tell Frederico. Sarah!'

She turned at the sound of agitation in Carlos's voice. 'You're sure you're OK to continue working? That was a difficult position you had to hold, crouched over your patient as we rushed down the corridor. I was worried about you. I've got the staffing situation under control now so if you need to—'

'I'm fine! Don't worry, Carlos.'

'If you say so. See you later!'

Later! For an instant Sarah allowed her thoughts to dwell on the evening ahead. She was as excited as a lovesick teenager with a crush on her teacher! But she mustn't think about it yet.

'How are you feeling now, Francesca?' she asked the small girl, who was now propped up against the pillows.

'*Gellato*,' the girl said. 'I want some ice cream.'

Sarah smiled as she turned to look at Francesca's mother. 'I would say your daughter is making a remarkable recovery.'

The mother smiled back. 'I'd promised Francesca some ice cream before she became ill.'

'And she shall have some up on the children's ward as soon as I can secure a bed for her. I'd like to admit Francesca for more tests. She'll probably need to be treated with antihistamine for a while. But don't worry. Research has shown that many children grow out of their allergies.'

'I hope that's true for Francesca.' The mother smiled as she stroked her daughter's hair. '*Grazie, Dottore.*'

Carlos checked Frederico's X-rays once again on the light box. This was without doubt one of the most badly damaged legs he'd seen in a long time. He traced his fingers over the smashed head of femur, totally dislocated from the acetabulum, before pointing out the splintered fracture in the midshaft area of the femur.

He glanced across at the orthopaedic consultant. 'What's the verdict?'

Carlos had been impressed with Vittorio Vincenzi's work ever since he'd started work at the hospital a couple of weeks ago. He'd been extremely co-operative with the staff in Pronto Soccorso, always making a point of answering their emergency calls if he wasn't in the middle of a major operation.

Vittorio raised an eyebrow. 'I'm going to take Frederico down to Theatre as soon as I can get my team together. In about a couple of hours, so nothing by mouth.'

Carlos nodded. 'You haven't answered my question, Vittorio. I know Frederico is going down to Theatre, but is the leg viable?'

'I may be able to screw and plate the femur, replace the head of femur and sort out the rest of the leg injuries. Or I may have to amputate. I can't tell at this stage. Were you thinking along those lines, Carlos?'

'Well, those are the alternatives, I would say,' Carlos answered cautiously.

Vittorio hesitated. 'I'll let you know when I've spent some time investigating the injuries.'

The orthopaedic consultant's expression didn't change. Carlos had noticed before that Vittorio was a completely unemotional person. A good trait in an excellent surgeon, but there was some underlying factor that was missing. He felt instinctively that the man had suffered some deep trauma, but he wasn't one to pry. Vittorio had been chosen by the hospital board of governors from many highly qualified applicants and he'd already made a good impression on his colleagues.

'I've left Frederico's wife with the obstetrics team in Theatre,' Carlos said. 'She's having a Caesarean at the moment. They're going to keep me informed but if Frederico asks after his wife it would be better not to tell him any details yet.'

Vittorio nodded. 'Don't worry, I can handle it, Carlos.'

'I'm sure you can.'

Carlos left X-Ray, leaving Vittorio to organise a bed for Frederico in the orthopaedic unit.

* * *

'So, how was your day, Sarah?'

Sarah smiled up at Carlos as he walked towards her in the reception area.

'Oh, fairly uneventful really. Violetta had a little boy. Did you hear about that?'

Carlos smiled back as he looked down at Sarah. She was looking particularly radiant tonight. Not a trace of weariness in spite of the fact that she was four months pregnant and had been working hard all day. She was wearing that delightful, pastel pink jacket and skirt he liked so much. She'd told him it was a size larger than she normally bought.

'I did hear about the Caesarean, Sarah. The obstetrics team informed me as a matter of course. And I was also asked to convey their thanks for the way the new English doctor prevented the premature birth and probable asphyxiation of the baby.'

'All in a day's work, *Dottore*,' Sarah said lightly, although she was feeling intensely relieved at the satisfactory outcome of the case.

She'd been petrified that Violetta was going to lose her baby! It had been difficult to stay relatively calm and focussed when all the odds had been stacked against them. It was ironic that so many of her friends had remarked how confident she always seemed in an emergency situation. Rubbish! She was only human. And in spite of her training and experience, every emergency posed an enormous challenge to her. She was always relieved when the outcome was favourable.

'They're keeping the baby in an incubator for a while,' Carlos said, placing an arm around Sarah as he guided her towards the revolving doors. 'He wasn't due for another six weeks but the team is confident he'll survive.'

Sarah smiled. 'The baby is gorgeous! I went up to the

premature babies' unit to have a look at the new arrival myself. Then I went to see Violetta to tell her that her little boy is making good progress. She's very tired but she's relieved that they've all survived the car crash.'

'Yes. Apparently a lorry came through the crash barrier and went into the side of their car. They're lucky to be alive.'

'How's Frederico?'

Carlos frowned. 'The orthopaedic team is operating at the moment. Vittorio tells me it's going to be a long operation. I hope they don't have to amputate.'

Sarah gave a little shiver. 'So do I. He's so young. Only nineteen. Violetta's eighteen. They've been married nearly a year. Violetta said Frederico was over the moon when she fell pregnant. I can imagine what it must have been like for a young couple who were so much in love…'

She broke off. She was getting these romantic ideas again. Maybe it was a reaction to the way she'd had to stay focussed all day.

Well, there was no harm in pretending to be a carefree teenager for the evening. Especially when she was going out with the most drop-dead gorgeous man in the whole of Rome!

CHAPTER SEVEN

'So, WHERE are we going tonight?' Sarah asked as she settled herself in the passenger seat of Carlos's steel-grey sports car.

She couldn't think why he wanted to drive through the Rome traffic and then struggle to find a parking place when it would be much easier to take a taxi. Maybe they were going somewhere on the outskirts of Rome where it was easier to park.

'We're going to a charity event concert,' Carlos said in a nonchalant voice as he acknowledged the wave of the porter on duty at the gate of the hospital.

'Really?'

'Oh, don't sound so disappointed! Pietro Mendicci puts on a very good show on these occasions.'

'Pietro Mendicci…you mean Judy's father?'

Carlos nodded. 'The very same. You'll be able to catch up with Judy. I hear she's enjoying life in Rome and hasn't suffered any asthma attacks since she arrived.'

'Good. I suspected that her asthma might have been brought on by stress. Obviously Pietro is being an attentive and understanding father.'

'Yes, and Judy's stepmother is treating Judy as if she were one of her own children, I believe. I met her when I was down at the coast this weekend, but you'll be able to judge for yourself this evening.'

'You don't mean we're going down to the coast this evening? I know you can drive fast but—'

'Less than an hour's drive, that's all, once we get out of Rome. I bought the tickets when I was down there over the weekend, though I was not sure what I was going to do with them. They were for a worthy cause, so I felt I had to support Pietro. When you and I were talking together this morning, I suddenly thought how nice it would be to go down and enjoy the concert in Pietro's beautiful garden.'

'But what time does it finish? I'm on early duty tomorrow.'

'Not any more! Your boss has changed the duty roster.'

Carlos smiled as he moved out into the fast lane. The road ahead was clear of traffic. They would make good time.

'But why have you suddenly sprung all this on me?'

Carlos took one hand off the wheel and closed his fingers around Sarah's hand. 'I've been thinking you looked as if you needed a break. A night by the sea will—'

Sarah gasped. 'You didn't say we were going to stay the night down there! I haven't brought even a toothbrush!'

Carlos was enjoying himself. 'A toothbrush! How very English, worrying about minor details. Don't worry, I can find you a new one. And you can have one of the new bathrooms that's in working order.'

'You mean we're going to stay at Villa Florissa?'

'It's only a couple of kilometres from Pietro's house. Very convenient.'

Sarah leaned back against her seat and closed her eyes. She was unsure how this evening was going to end. She couldn't help wishing that Carlos had warned her she was going to be spending the night in the villa where she'd been so happy as a child. But perhaps she might have become too apprehensive about the situation.

Carlos's manner towards her had been changing during the day. Even though they'd been busy, there had been a certain underlying emotion that had kept coming through whenever they'd been near each other. And when he'd kissed her hand that morning he'd seemed charged with electricity. As if he'd come to an important decision regarding their future together perhaps?

She felt a tremor of delicious anticipation running through her as she remembered the feel of his lips on her skin. Had Carlos planned to bring her down to the coast because his feelings for her were becoming more clear?

She would find out later! But for the moment she was simply going to imagine that Carlos felt as she did. That the two of them could have an enjoyable evening together. Meanwhile, she planned to relax in her comfortable seat as the car purred its way along the road to the coast.

'Carlos, I'm so glad you were able to come.'

An attractive, slim, dark-haired lady in a well-cut cream silk evening gown kissed Carlos on each cheek. Sarah glanced around her at the well-heeled guests who were strolling in the garden, chatting smiling, sipping their drinks. In the gathering twilight, it made an interesting scene. So typically Italian! Sarah loved the visual effect of the many coloured dresses floating across the manicured lawn.

She glanced down at her pale pink suit, wishing she could transform it into one of those beautiful gowns. Italian women certainly knew how to dress for the occasion. And those fantastic stiletto heels that she would find impossible to walk on!

She noticed a couple of younger women who were wearing jackets and skirts so perhaps her outfit would merge in after all.

The hostess was now holding out her hand towards Sarah.

'Do introduce me to your charming companion, Carlos.'

'Mariana, this is Dr Sarah Montgomery, a colleague and dear friend from England.'

'You must be the wonderful lady who took care of my

stepdaughter on the plane. All the children have been bathed ready for bed and they're in their rooms. I know Judy would be disappointed not to see you. Would you like me to take you upstairs for a few minutes?'

'I'd like that very much.'

'We will be back very soon,' Mariana said, waving to one of the waiters who was carrying a drinks tray. 'Help yourself to a drink, Carlos.'

Sarah was impressed with the elegance of the large Mendicci house as she walked up the broad staircase.

'The children have an entire wing of the house,' Mariana explained as they walked along the landing. 'Pietro and I have five children and now that Pietro's delightful daughter has joined the family we need lots of space for them to play.'

'Sarah!' Judy, sitting up in the frilly, counterpaned bed of her pink, yellow and cream-coloured bedroom, put down her book and held out her arms. 'I didn't know you were coming.'

Sarah leaned down to be hugged enthusiastically. 'I didn't know I was coming until we started driving down here.'

She turned to look at her bejewelled hostess in her expensive looking gown as she switched back to Italian. 'I didn't know I was coming here, which is why I'm not sure if I'm suitably dressed for this evening.'

'You look absolutely charming! Your little suit shows off your slim young figure to perfection.'

Sarah smiled. She'd put on a few pounds but apparently it didn't show yet. But not for much longer!

'Now, if you'll excuse me, Sarah, I'd better go and circulate with my guests. Come down as soon as you've finished your conversation with Judy.' Mariana bent down to kiss her stepdaughter and spoke in charmingly accented

English. 'You must allow Sarah to leave you soon, Judy, OK?'

Judy smiled happily as she kissed her stepmother.

Sarah chatted for a few minutes with Judy, pleased to see how content her little patient now was, before kissing her goodbye and returning to the garden. As she walked across the lawn, she was thinking how fortunate it was that Judy had been totally integrated here with the rest of the Mendicci children.

Carlos smiled as he left the group he'd been talking to and came towards Sarah.

'Was Judy still awake?'

Sarah nodded. 'Very much. We had a nice long chat and she confided that she's very happy she's going to live here permanently. She doesn't want to go back to England because she hates the man her mother has just married. He sounds like a most unpleasant character so Judy is much better off here. And she's having no problem learning to speak Italian. Not with five step-siblings to help her! Judy's mother has agreed to let Judy stay with Pietro and Mariana permanently, but she's promised to visit whenever she can.'

'Good. I suppose Judy's mother will not have much time to spare when the new baby arrives but at least Judy is now part of a family that is totally reliable.'

Carlos linked hands with Sarah as they strolled towards the long buffet table set out under the trees.

There were cold meats, oysters, shrimps, prawns and salads of every kind. With their laden plates, they sat down at one of the smaller tables dotted around the garden. Lights shining from the trees illuminated the garden.

Pietro came over to talk to them for a while, before he had to go across to the stage and announce that the performance was about to begin.

A small group of musicians began to play the overture to Puccini's *Madame Butterfly*.

'I love this opera,' Sarah whispered to Carlos. 'It's a very small stage so I presume it's a concert performance, not a full performance of the opera.'

Carlos nodded. 'We're going to hear excerpts from *Madame Butterfly*. The soloists are singers who perform at the leading opera houses in Italy.'

Throughout the performance, Sarah was thrilled at the excellence of the singing. She was also very moved. As the lovely young soprano sang Madame Butterfly's final aria, '*Un Bel di Vedremo—One Fine Day*'—Sarah had to hold back the tears.

Madame Butterfly, watching her lover's ship draw ever nearer, was confident that he was returning to make her his wife. She was longing to show him the son she'd borne him during his absence. But she didn't know that her lover was already married to someone else. Yes, he was returning to claim his son, but he planned to take him away from her...

Carlos took hold of her hand. She turned to look at him. In the shimmering lights coming from the stage she could see his emotionally charged expression. Was the tenderness in his eyes for her or for the poignant story being enacted on the stage?

She glanced up at the moon shining down on the rapt audience as the opera drew to its poignant, heartbreaking denouement, making a silent prayer that her own situation would have a happier conclusion.

The car was nearing the Villa Florissa, turning in through the wide open gates.

Sarah smiled. 'That's new, having electronically controlled gates. How impressive! I was always the one who had to get out of the car and open the gates.'

'You'll be amazed by the changes we've made.'

'I'm sure I will.' She hesitated. 'Is your mother in residence at your house next door? I have to say, I'm a bit apprehensive about meeting her again.'

'Oh, didn't I tell you? My parents are back in Rome.'

'Carlos, you know you didn't tell me!'

'How wicked of me. Whatever must you be thinking?'

'I'm thinking how relieved I am!'

'I thought you might be.' Carlos held open the car door.

She glanced up at the imposing façade of the old stone villa as she walked up to the huge front door. So many memories were flooding back. It was as if the place was haunted by ghosts from the past.

'You've got lots of lights on in the house. It certainly looks lived in.'

'I've had all the lights put on time switches. I can activate some of them when I open the gates.'

'Amazing! You're a technological genius!'

'I know. Come inside.'

He led her through to the sitting room, which had long casement windows opening on to the lawn. Carlos pushed open the windows.

'I'm going to have a drink. What would you like to drink, Sarah?'

'Something with fruit.'

Carlos laughed. 'You mean one of those concoctions we had in the wine bar last week? A glass full of green leaves with segments of orange swimming around in fruit juice?'

Sarah grinned. 'Well, a modification of that would be lovely.'

She stretched out on the sofa and looked out through the casement windows at the moonlit garden. It was after midnight but she didn't feel at all tired. Excited, exhilarated, but definitely not tired.

They sipped their drinks as they sat in companionable silence. Sarah had curled her feet under her so that Carlos could sit beside her on the sofa.

She finished her drink and put it on a place mat on the highly polished oak coffee-table she remembered so well.

'Can you see that mark on the wood, Carlos? That's where I dropped that heavy pebble I'd brought up from the beach for my mother. Instead of thanking me, she was furious! I got some polish and tried to disguise the dent in the surface but it wouldn't disappear.'

Carlos smiled. 'I remember that particular episode. My mother wasn't too pleased about it either.'

He stood up and held out his hands towards her. 'Come on, it's time I took you upstairs. You and Charlotte need your beauty sleep.'

Sarah smiled. It was lovely to hear Carlos saying her daughter's name. It made her realise how lucky she was to be looking forward to having a daughter. Another lifelong friend, but this time her own flesh and blood. She took hold of Carlos's outstretched hands and let him draw her towards him. She expected him to release her when she was standing in front of him but his hands remained tightly clasped around hers. Their bodies were almost touching.

She drew in her breath as he put his arms around her and drew her against him. Looking up into his eyes, she could see the tenderness that had been there during those last poignant moments of Madame Butterfly's final aria. Yes, he'd been moved by the music as she had, but it was obvious now that some of the tenderness she'd seen in his expression had been directed towards her.

Slowly, oh, so slowly, Carlos lowered his head and kissed her with consummate gentleness on the lips. She found herself relaxing into the rhythm of his body. She could feel his heart beating against her breasts as she realised that she was longing for more than an embrace. Much more! Her body had never felt so alive, so ready to respond…so desperately yearning to make love…

Even as the thought came to her, she tensed. She mustn't

allow herself to relax. If she let down her guard and became too involved, she would be too frustrated to sleep!

She tried to move away, but Carlos was holding her firmly in his arms.

'Darling, what's the matter?'

'You don't have to be kind to me, Carlos. I can—'

'Kind! Is that what you think this is? This has nothing to do with kindness. I love you, Sarah. I think I always have. It was different, of course, when you were just a child, but now—'

'Carlos, I'm pregnant! You may think you love me…but you can't possibly find me sexually attractive any more. I mean…you don't want to make love to me, do you?'

Carlos pretended to give the question some serious thought before he couldn't hold back his rakish grin. 'Was that an invitation?'

Sarah's heart leapt in response to the way he'd made a play on her words. She'd been giving him an excuse to opt out but, instead of taking it, he'd turned it around in the most wonderfully exciting way.

She smiled coquettishly. 'My question wasn't meant to be an invitation. It could be…but I'll need persuading if…'

Carlos had already swept her up into his arms and was heading for the staircase. At the corner of the stairs he paused to kiss her.

She clung to him, revelling in the taste of his lips, the vibrancy of his athletic body pressed against her. This was her idea of heaven! She wasn't going to think of the consequences. Tonight they were young lovers and tomorrow didn't exist…

Carlos pushed open the door to the room where he always slept when he came down to the villa. Gently he laid his precious Sarah down on the bed, before drawing back the sheets.

Sarah began stripping off her clothes, tossing them onto

the carpet, anxious that the erotic mood she'd started down-stairs wouldn't disappear. She wanted so much to lose her-self in Carlos's arms. She didn't want this sensual rapport between them to vanish.

Carlos's breathing was ragged as he dragged his shirt over his head. Buttons took too long…

Gently, caressing Sarah, he eased her between the sheets, cocooned her in a loving embrace before kissing her slowly, maddeningly too slowly for both of them, but he didn't want to rush these magic moments…

He'd never before felt so aroused. He realised that Sarah was his ultimate dream. There'd never been anyone in his life to compare with her. And now here she was in his arms.

'I've never made love to a pregnant woman before,' he whispered as he nibbled her ear lobe. 'I know I'm a doctor but you'll have to tell me if you feel any kind of discom-fort.'

'Carlos, the only kind of discomfort I'm feeling is my insatiable longing for you. Oh, please, Carlos. Don't caress me in that tantalising way…it's too…no, no…'

Why was she saying no when she meant yes, yes…?

But Carlos intuitively knew exactly what she meant.

'Carlos, I can't hold out any longer. Please, please…'

Sarah's voice ended in a desperate moan as she pleaded for Carlos to take her completely. His caresses had been fun…then exciting…then too stimulatingly erotic for her to contain her impatience for consummation.

'Yes, yes… Ahh!—'

She moaned ecstatically as she drifted off into a paradise where only she and Carlos existed…

The morning sun was shining on the window-sill. Sarah could hear the sound of the birds singing in the garden. She'd never felt so deliriously happy! She turned on her side, and as she looked at Carlos, sleeping beside her, she realised that she'd fallen in love with him soon after she'd started work at the Ospedale Tevere. And now her love had deepened into the sort of magical experience she hadn't known existed. Did she dare to hope that it might continue like this for ever?

For ever was a long time! Now she really was wishing for the moon. There were far too many obstacles to overcome before she could start thinking about a permanent romantic relationship with Carlos. Her baby, for instance! Dear little Charlotte, who seemed to have slept through the whole of last night without giving her mum the slightest problem.

Sarah leaned back against the pillows and closed her eyes again as she remembered how gentle Carlos had been when they'd made love. His caresses had driven her wild with desire. She'd been longing for consummation. And when he'd entered her, oh, so gently at first and then with a rhythmic, tantalising pulse, she'd cried out in ecstasy.

She opened her eyes again as she felt Carlos stirring beside her. He reached out and drew her into the circle of his arms.

'Did I waken you, Sarah?'

'I was already awake. I was…I was thinking about how wonderful it was…to make love with you. I never thought it would happen because…because, being pregnant…'

'Being pregnant makes no difference. If anything, you seem even more desirable to me. Being a bit more rounded suits you.'

Sarah laughed as she patted her plump waistline. 'Is that what I am, rounded?'

Carlos caressed her abdomen gently. 'You will be. You're going to look like one of those gorgeous, sensually desirable ladies that Rubens used to paint.'

'Well, if I'm going to look gorgeous and desirable, I can't wait!'

Carlos hesitated, taking care to phrase his feelings in a way that wouldn't cause Sarah any distress. They usually spoke English when they were alone together and sometimes he found it difficult to choose the right words.

'I have to admit that when you first told me you were pregnant I found it difficult to come to terms with the fact that you were carrying another man's child. But now…'

'What made you change?' Sarah asked quickly. 'It was something that happened yesterday, I'm sure.'

Carlos leaned back against his pillows, one arm encircling her shoulder as again he chose his words even more carefully.

Sarah waited apprehensively for him to continue. They may have made wonderful love together last night but their relationship was still very fragile.

'Sarah, since I knew you were pregnant, I felt I had no right to make love with you. I even felt that, because you were carrying Robin's child, you in some way belonged to him.'

Sarah moved closer, reaching up to kiss Carlos on the cheek. He swallowed hard.

'I think…yesterday…you finally convinced me that Robin is never going to be a real father to Charlotte. I realised that I was worrying too much about Robin coming to claim you and his child. But that's not going to happen…is it?'

'No, it's not. But I can understand why you felt like that,' Sarah said quietly. 'Charlotte isn't your child but—'

'After last night, being so close to you, I feel as if she is. I fervently wish she were my child. But she is…' He hesitated, again searching for the right words. 'I now think of her as my own child because you're her mother and I love you deeply, Sarah. After she's born, I'm going to love this child as if she were my own…if you'll let me,' he added cautiously.

'Oh, Carlos! There's nothing I'd like better. I wish you were her real father.' She broke off. Now she was fighting back the tears.

'Does that mean you'd accept me as surrogate father to Charlotte?'

Sarah nodded, unable to speak because of her turbulent emotions. She'd wished that Carlos had been the father of her unborn child. It was almost as if her wish was coming true.

Carlos turned his head to look at Sarah. 'I suppose it's a good thing we're both doctors. During the night, when we made love, I knew that I had to be more careful than...than I might have been if I'd allowed myself to lose control.'

'Carlos, you were wonderful!' Sarah snuggled against him. 'You were so—'

'If you snuggle up in that sexy way, you'll have to realise that you're being far too provocative for a man who's madly in love with you. I'm not made of stone.'

Carlos raised himself on one elbow to look down at her. 'I don't want to tire you, especially in your delicate condition, but—'

'Carlos, I'm desperate to make love again. I'm not going to break in two if you—'

As Carlos's kiss silenced her she gave herself up to the wonderful feeling of anticipation...excitement...longing... and finally fulfilment that consumed her, transporting her to another planet where the problems of everyday life were swept away...

Sitting beside Carlos on the way back to Rome she felt as if she was floating on cloud nine. To all intents and purposes the child she was carrying now belonged to both of them. Robin had, in effect, opted out of his responsibilities, as she'd expected he would. Carlos had asked to be surrogate father to Charlie and that was what they both wanted. It was her dream come true.

She turned sideways to look at his handsome profile in the slanting rays of the late afternoon sunlight. She wondered fleetingly how the rest of their medical colleagues viewed her relationship with Carlos. She hadn't actually told anybody yet that she was pregnant, but she knew she would soon have to break the news. She had the feeling that one of the nurses in Obstetrics might have already divulged the information that Sarah was having antenatal care.

'Carlos, I'm going to have to let everybody know I'm pregnant soon,' she said evenly. 'I'm not quite sure how they'll take it. When they ask me who the father is…'

'They won't,' Carlos said quietly.

He cursed as he was forced to slam on the brakes to avoid a car that was pulling out into the fast lane without indicating. Regaining his composure, he moved forward again.

'Sarah, you're from England. You haven't been here long enough to make close friendships with any of the staff. They might take a guess at who the father is but they won't pry.'

'And if they took a guess, what would they come up with?'

Carlos took one hand off the wheel and squeezed Sarah's. 'I would be honoured if they thought that Charlotte was mine.'

Sarah looked out of the window as Carlos turned off the autostrada, steering the car slowly through the noisy, rush-hour traffic in central Rome.

'I think you've sussed out my way of thinking,' she said carefully. 'I have to admit that when I was choosing a name for our daughter…I mean my daughter…'

'Our daughter,' Carlos corrected. 'I love to hear you say it.'

Sarah smiled. 'I'll say it again if you like. Our daughter, our daughter Charlotte. It sounds wonderful. But if anyone actually asks who Charlie's father is, I'll have to tell them the truth.'

'Of course! So long as we feel as if we're Charlotte's parents, that's all that matters.'

They were driving along the bank of the river. The sun's rays were slanting on the water. Carlos turned the car into the hospital.

'Would you like to go out for supper tonight?'

Sarah nodded happily. 'Early supper, please. Charlotte and I are starving!'

Carlos leaned across and kissed her lightly on the lips.

'We'll go out as soon as you can make it.'

Sarah went into her room and sat down on the edge of the bed. What a difference a day had made! Yesterday morning she had felt so despondent about her relationship with Carlos. But now...

It was as if they were a married couple, looking forward to the birth of their first child.

A tiny voice inside her head began nagging her. Don't let down your guard or become too complacent. Your relationship with Carlos is just too good to last. There's so much that could happen between now and the birth of your baby...

CHAPTER EIGHT

DURING the next few weeks, Sarah felt a sense of well-being and happiness that she'd never experienced before. She knew that it was partly because, after the first couple of months of suffering morning sickness, she was now sailing through her pregnancy with no complications, as she'd hoped. But it was mostly due to the fact that she was so desperately in love with Carlos. She felt like a teenager having her first love affair, as if she didn't have a care in the world!

Nothing worried her any more in either her personal or professional life. She found that even when she was physically tired at the end of a long day in Accident and Emergency, her spirits never drooped. A quick shower, a change of clothes and she was ready to go out and explore the interesting areas of Rome with Carlos.

Ever since they'd spent their night together in the Villa Florissa and Carlos had said that he felt as if he was a father-to-be, it seemed that nothing could spoil their relationship. At the end of many of their evenings together, Sarah would sleep with Carlos. Sometimes they would make love, gently, tenderly, both of them always conscious of Sarah's condition but poignantly aware that their love for each other was growing stronger each time they were together.

One warm May evening as they sat beside the Trevi Fountain, enjoying the last rays of the sun, Carlos told Sarah he'd never been so happy in the whole of his life.

He tossed a coin into the water, then another one. Sarah tossed a third coin.

'Three coins in the fountain,' Sarah murmured. 'I ought to make a wish, but I don't need to wish for anything more than I already have.'

Carlos put one hand on the still warm stone surrounding the Trevi Fountain as he leaned across to kiss Sarah gently on the lips. It didn't matter that they were surrounded by other people. There was always an air of romance here by the cooling spray of the fountain.

The lights nearby were causing an iridescent sheen to appear over the surface of the surrounding pool and as the fountain jets sprayed out they gave a rainbow effect that hung in the fragrant springtime air. Young couples spending a couple of days in Rome together were vowing to love each other for ever.

Tonight Carlos felt there was magic in the air. He and Sarah were another young couple, completely in love with each other, with a wonderful future ahead of them.

'I feel exactly as you do, Sarah,' he said huskily as he caressed her hand. 'There's nothing more I could wish for. But I'll make a wish anyway.' He smiled lovingly down at her. 'Let me see, there must be something I need… I won't tell you what it is because it's got to be a secret…'

Sarah closed her eyes and thought of something she wanted. She silently wished that nothing would happen to spoil her relationship with Carlos and that they would be together for ever.

As she opened her eyes she saw that Carlos was watching her with concerned eyes.

'I've got to go away at the beginning of July for a couple of weeks.'

He paused. Sarah waited. She didn't want Carlos to go away but she would cope for a couple of weeks.

'A year ago, I was booked to speak at a medical conference in Milan. At that time I didn't even know you would be here in Rome with me or that—'

'Or that I would be pregnant and you would be worrying about leaving me alone. Carlos, I'll be fine. I work in a hospital and—'

'That's another thing I worry about. Having you work with me in Pronto Soccorso. It's the most difficult department in the hospital. Nobody can predict what's going to happen from one day to the next. I've seen you having to physically restrain some of our more difficult patients. The tourists who get drunk are the worst. Sarah, promise me you'll call me if—'

'Carlos, I don't need to call you. You're always there, the moment I begin to feel threatened.' She paused. 'And I love you for it,' she added softly.

'Yes, but I won't be there for the first two weeks in July. You'll be nearly seven months pregnant.'

'And I'll be surrounded by experienced and well trained A and E doctors and nurses! Nothing will go wrong. I presume you've appointed a deputy.'

Carlos nodded. 'Vittorio Vincenzi is going to be in charge of the department. So if you have any problems…'

'I'll refer them to Vittorio,' Sarah reassured him.

She leaned across and kissed Carlos. 'Please, don't worry about me. I'll miss you terribly while you're away but just think of our reunion. When do you get back from the conference?'

Carlos pulled out his diary. 'July fifteenth.'

'My birthday! My thirtieth birthday. And my last day at work before I take my maternity leave. Oh, Carlos, you've got to be there. Lucy arrives in the afternoon to take over from me for three months. So I'm planning a party in the evening for some of my friends and colleagues and—'

'Ask somebody to help you with the party,' Carlos said quickly. 'Helena would be useful because she knows what a seven-months-pregnant thirty-year-old can and can't do.'

Sarah smiled. 'Carlos, I'll be fine. Just make sure you get back in time to enjoy the fun.'

As they walked back through the streets, Sarah had one of her occasional feelings of misgiving. As quickly as it arose she dismissed the unpleasant thought. She knew she could cope with her difficult work in Pronto Soccorso. Her pregnancy didn't make any difference. Everything was going smoothly.

But as the weather got hotter during June and her body increased in size, Sarah found herself becoming more tired, especially when they were busy in the department and she had no time for a break during the day.

At the beginning of July, Carlos made it clear that he thought Sarah was working too hard. Sarah was well aware that Carlos didn't really want to leave her for a couple of weeks to go to the conference in Milan. He was constantly referring to it, questioning whether to cancel so that he could remain with her in Rome. She'd had to state categorically that the conference was more important than she was. It was a brilliant career step to be recognised as an international expert on accident and emergency techniques. He simply had to go!

But one afternoon when Sarah had been very busy all morning and hadn't had time for lunch, she was confronted by a particularly difficult patient. Jeff, a strong, muscular English tourist, over in Rome with a group of construction workers, had been on a two-day binge and had drunk more than had been good for him. He'd got into a fight with another man in the group he was travelling with and had ended up with a stab wound in his leg.

As he'd hobbled into Pronto Soccorso, dripping blood, cursing and swearing, Sarah had taken him straight to the nearest empty cubicle. The paperwork could come later. This man needed immediate attention. But as she attempted to clean up the wound, Jeff became abusive, demanding that Sarah get him another drink.

'I'm on whisky and soda, darling. Easy on the soda, it's bad for my liver—Oh, hell!'

The patient leaned precariously over the edge of the examination couch as Sarah grabbed a vomit bowl.

Just in time! She waited till he'd finished, wiping his mouth, before holding a glass of water to his lips.

'Sip it slowly, Jeff. That's right. Gently does it.'

Her patient grimaced but took a few tentative sips before collapsing back on the couch and falling into an alcohol-induced sleep. With Jeff snoring loudly, Sarah continued with her treatment of his leg. The wound wasn't as extensive as she'd feared. Once she'd cleaned away the congealed blood she was able to begin suturing the wound.

She glanced up as Carlos came into the cubicle. He looked worried.

'I heard the noise. Are you OK, Sarah?'

'I'm fine! My patient will sleep for a long time now so I can get on with job.'

She continued putting in the stitches, intensely aware that Carlos was still anxious. She was trying desperately to look bright and alert even though her back was beginning to ache. She didn't want to worry Carlos. He was constantly making sure that she took care of herself.

He leaned against the side of the examination couch. 'Have you had a lunch-break?'

Sarah was carefully pulling the edges of the wound together as she put in the vital stitch that would hold the middle section.

'There! That should hold it. Another five or six stitches and—'

'Sarah, have you had any lunch?' Carlos repeated patiently.

She took a deep breath. 'I haven't had time for lunch, Carlos. When I've finished suturing this wound, I'll—'

'I'll finish that.' Carlos was already scrubbing his hands at the sink. 'Go and have lunch and take the rest of the day off, please.'

Hearing Carlos using his most authoritative, professional no-nonsense voice, she knew better than to argue.

She put down her needle and peeled off her gloves. As she looked across at Carlos she thought how handsome he looked when he was being masterful! Her resentment fizzled away. As usual, Carlos was simply concerned that she wasn't taking care of herself…or rather taking care of herself and her unborn child.

The precious child that he now thought of as his own.

Carlos was pulling on a pair of sterile gloves. He leaned over the sleeping patient, who was still snoring loudly.

'Beautiful embroidery, Sarah,' he observed, before looking across at her as she paused by the door. 'Now, will you go away or do I have to—?'

'I'm going!'

Picking up some bread, cheese and an orange from the canteen, Sarah decided to go to her room and put her feet up. It was rest she needed more than food.

She stretched out on her bed and swallowed some bread and cheese, washing it down with a glass of mineral water. Her eyes felt heavy. She was so tired that the drone of the traffic outside was soothing rather than disturbing. She would have a few minutes' snooze and then…

She awoke to find Carlos sitting on the edge of her bed, looking at her with a deeply concerned expression.

'You were seriously overtired,' he said, as he bent to kiss her. 'It never even registers with you that it's time for a break, does it? Sarah, I'm worried about you.'

She raised herself into a sitting position.

'Carlos, I'm healthier than I've ever been! It's only the extra weight that makes me tired sometimes. Alessandro is delighted with my progress. You saw that picture of my scan last week. Look, it's here somewhere—let me show you again, just to remind you how healthy we both are.'

Proudly, she lifted up the precious picture from her bedside table. 'You can see that everything's fine. Look, there's her dear little head…and that's a well-formed hand—see the fingers! Charlotte's growing at a normal rate and—'

'Darling, she's beautiful! And, yes, I know everything is normal. But you're nearly seven months pregnant. What isn't normal is the fact that you're still working full time.'

'Carlos, lots of women work full time! Some of them work until the time their baby is due to be born.'

'But, Sarah, you're working in Pronto Soccorso, a very demanding department where you're on your feet all day. Sometimes you have to use physical strength to cope with a difficult patient—like today. I could hear you were having trouble. I was coping with a very demanding patient myself at the time or I would have come immediately to help you. I don't want you to lose our baby! I think you should—'

'Carlos, I'm not going to lose our baby. Charlotte is in excellent condition and she's perfectly safe. Yes, I get tired but—'

Carlos cleared his throat. 'Sarah, I'd like you to consider working part time until you start your maternity leave in a couple of weeks. I'm going to be away at the conference in Milano for the next two weeks and I don't want to think of you getting overtired while I'm away. Mornings only would make sense, don't you think?'

Sarah hesitated. She had to admit that the prospect was very appealing and she didn't like to see Carlos looking so worried about her.

'Look, Carlos, I know that I'm fit enough to continue

working full time, but if you find it worrying to watch me…'

'I do find it worrying! I'd rather draft in extra staff than have you making yourself overtired, missing your lunch and generally not taking care of yourself as you did today.'

'OK, OK, you've made your point. It's kind of you to be so concerned.'

Carlos ran a hand through his dark hair.

'There you go again, calling me kind! Just as you did the first time I was intent on seducing you.' He gave her a rakish grin. 'As I told you then, kindness has got nothing to do with my feelings for you. Oh, Sarah…my precious Sarah…'

He lay down on the narrow bed beside her, drawing her into the circle of his arms, nuzzling her neck, revelling in the scent of her body, the unusually plump contours of her curvaceous body.

'You are so very precious to me… I love you so much…'

He kissed her gently on the lips while one hand was gently caressing her abdomen. Suddenly, he broke off.

'I do believe Charlotte kicked me just then! Yes, she's definitely moving. Sarah, put your hand here…'

Sarah laughed. 'I can feel Charlotte from the inside, remember? And she's having a dancing session at the moment. Ouch!'

Sarah moved away to ease herself into a more comfortable position.

Carlos began laughing as he clung to the side of the bed.

'There's not room for the three of us in this narrow bed any more. That's another thing I wanted to talk to you about.'

He sat up on the side of the bed, leaning over Sarah so that he could put one arm around her shoulders.

'I'd like you to move out of this little room and—'

'Carlos, I know what you're going to say again, but I don't want to move into your room. I need my own space and I'd like to keep this place. I spend most nights in your room any way, so it's not going to make any difference, is it?'

'I don't want you to move into my room, Sarah. When I get back from Milano, I'd like you to move into our apartment here in Rome.'

Sarah stared at Carlos in amazement. 'You mean, move in with your mother and father? You can't be serious! Your mother would be scandalised.'

'My parents have moved back to our house on the coast. My mother's decided she's tired of city life. They've given me the apartment in Rome and I intend to move there after the conference.'

'So we'd have the apartment to ourselves, would we?' Sarah said.

'We certainly would. You would be on maternity leave. You could have a relaxing day and then be ready for a fun evening with me when I get home.'

Sarah smiled. 'Well, put like that, it sounds very tempting. In fact, I'm definitely warming to the idea. Just so long as I don't make any marks on your mother's posh coffee-tables or break any of her antiques!'

'Sarah, it all belongs to me now, so you can do what you like. What do you say? Will you move in with me when I get back from Milano?'

'I'd love to.'

Carlos drew her against him, gently kissing the side of her cheek. 'You're so precious to me. I couldn't bear it if anything—'

Sarah's phone started ringing. She reached out one hand towards the bedside table to answer it.

'Robin!'

Her heart sank as she heard the unexpected but familiar

voice at the other end of the line. She'd been relieved that he hadn't phoned for a while and she'd been spared their emotionally charged discussions which led nowhere.

'Where are you, Robin? No, you can't be!'

She put a hand over the phone and stared aghast at Carlos. 'Robin says he's here in Rome. He wants to come and see me so that we can talk. Oh, Carlos, what shall I do?'

Carlos felt as if a cold hand was squeezing his heart. His worst nightmare was coming true. The man he'd hoped would disappear from Sarah's life was actually here in Rome. And that man had a legitimate right to everything that Carlos had hoped to make his own.

'You'll have to see him, Sarah,' Carlos said evenly. 'He's the father of your baby. You'd better make arrangements to meet.'

He stood up and began walking towards the door.

'Carlos, don't go. Don't leave me.'

Robin's voice could be heard on the line. 'Sarah, are you still there? What's happening your end? Have you got somebody with you?'

'No, I had but he's just left,' Sarah said despondently. 'We'd better arrange to meet. We need to talk.'

'Look, I'm in a cab, somewhere near your hospital. I got through to your switchboard and they gave me your room number. I'll pick you up in…say, ten minutes. In your reception area, OK?'

'Robin, I know we need to talk but not right now! I can't drop everything and—'

'Sorry, I missed that. The line's breaking up. Looking forward to seeing you in ten minutes.'

'Aagh!' Sarah cut the connection and glared down at her phone. The switchboard had no right to give out information about her room number.

Oh, yes, they had, said the sane little voice inside her

head. Robin is the father of your unborn baby. He has every right to contact you and check on his child's welfare.

Sarah groaned as she patted the precious mound beneath her heavy breasts.

'I'm sorry, Charlie, I know your father means well but honestly he couldn't have come at a worse time. Just when Carlos is leaving me for a couple of weeks. Just when we thought we had everything sorted for our future. You like Carlos, don't you? Yes, I can tell you do—but, then again, you've got to get to know your biological father as well…'

She broke off her conversation with her daughter. These precious exchanges between herself and Charlie had become more frequent. Well, she knew that babies in the womb responded to their mother's voices. But equally as important, she'd come to value her chats with Charlie, sharing her problems, explaining why something was going to happen. Sarah knew that anybody listening in to these conversations might think she'd flipped!

Maybe she had! No, it was all too real! Charlotte must surely be listening to her. Not understanding the words but getting the general idea that her mum was treading a delicate line between loving Carlos, wanting him to be around as the father of her child, while at the same time doing the correct and dutiful thing by Charlotte and her biological father.

Whatever else these dotty, hormonal conversations were, they were certainly a release of tension! She sincerely hoped they were of some value to her unborn child. Meanwhile, she really should get a move on if she was to meet Robin.

Why on earth hadn't the wretched man phoned to say he was coming? Why now when everything was running along so smoothly?

She pulled on the loose, flowing dress she'd bought last week when she'd discovered she'd gone up yet another dress size. Fastening the buttons over her bump, she began to feel nervous and apprehensive. Robin couldn't have changed, could he? Because he hadn't phoned for a while she'd assumed that he was being true to type. A more unpaternal type she couldn't imagine! Footloose and fancy-free didn't begin to describe Robin!

So why had he come to Rome? Italy was a long way from Africa. He surely wasn't planning to try his hand at full-time fatherhood, was he?

Suddenly she knew she didn't want to face Robin by herself. She needed help and there was only one person who could give her that.

After leaving Sarah, Carlos went to his room and closed the door. He could spare himself a few minutes before he went back to work. His department was relatively quiet at the moment and he had almost a full complement of experienced staff. The relative calm could change at any moment, but he would be contacted if he was needed.

He went to the fridge and poured himself a glass of mineral water, adding a few ice cubes to clink around. What he needed was a much stronger drink, but he never drank while he was on duty.

He swirled the ice round in his glass and lifted it to his lips. Why had Robin come to Rome? Why now, when everything was going so well between himself and Sarah?

Could it be that Robin had decided to shoulder his responsibilities?

Carlos groaned. Those very responsibilities that he himself had assumed. Oh, not out of duty...oh, no, taking care of Sarah could never be described as a duty. He loved her as if she were his wife, the mother of his child. And the little one they both knew as Charlotte or Charlie had become very precious to him.

He couldn't wait for the baby to be born! She would be

so cherished. He'd planned to be there at the birth. To hold Sarah's hand, wipe her face with cooling swabs, give her encouraging words, while Alessandro and his obstetrics team took charge of the delivery. He planned to make sure that all the staff were fully alert, watching for any possible complication. Sarah must have the best possible attention.

She'd confided in him that she wanted the delivery to be as natural as possible, but if she needed painkillers, an epidural or even a Caesarean, she would go along with what the obstetrics team recommended.

This baby, the baby he'd thought of as his own for the past few months, would be given a brilliant start in life. Nothing but the best was good enough for Sarah and Charlotte.

But now that Robin had turned up so unexpectedly, the whole scenario had changed. Carlos knew that he now had absolutely no right to expect any loyalty from Sarah or the child.

He began to pace the room. How did Sarah really feel towards Robin? She was carrying Robin's child. She must have felt something for him during the months they'd lived together as a couple. Nearly a year, apparently.

Had Sarah been in love with Robin? Was she perhaps still secretly in love with her former lover but feeling let down because of his seeming indifference? Had that love been rekindled on the night that Sarah had become pregnant?

Carlos swallowed hard. Sarah must have been a willing participant. The thought appalled him, but he realised he had to face the truth. It was only months since Sarah had become pregnant by Robin.

She would have to meet him fairly soon. Robin hadn't flown all the way from Africa to Italy to make a phone call. Why had he gone to all that trouble when he could simply have phoned from anywhere in the world? Maybe he still felt deeply about Sarah, especially now that she was carrying his child. Perhaps he was intent on resuming their relationship, if only for the sake of their child...

'No!'

Carlos stood up, whacking his hand against his forehead in frustration. It had all been going so well. Sarah had agreed to move into the apartment with him. He was planning to ask if she would marry him. He had every hope that she would agree. Their future together as a family unit had seemed assured but now...

He went into the bedroom and dragged a suitcase from the built in shelves above the wardrobe. He mustn't forget to prepare for his trip to Milano tomorrow. There would be no time to pack in the morning. It was going to be even more difficult to leave Sarah here in Rome now that Robin had arrived.

He walked quickly to the door. He would work all evening. Keep his mind off what was happening. He couldn't solve anything by torturing himself with images of what Robin meant to Sarah.

His phone rang. 'Sarah?' He took a deep breath to calm himself but his words tumbled out in his emotional agitation. 'Why are you calling me? I thought you'd be meeting Robin by now.'

'I'm down in Reception, waiting for him. Carlos, I...I'd like you to be with me when I meet Robin. I'm so confused. You feel more like Charlotte's father than Robin. Please, say you'll come and help me out.'

Sarah sounded as if she really needed him.

'I'll come, but only for a few minutes. You and Robin must sort out your own problems without me interfering.'

He hurried down to Reception in time to see Sarah walking across to greet a tall, fair-haired man who was coming in through the main entrance.

'Sarah…darling… Lord! You've put some weight on, haven't you? And how's my little…?'

Carlos stood still as he closed his eyes, unable to bear the sight of Robin putting his hand on Sarah's abdomen in a familiar, proprietorial way.

'Carlos!' Sarah had seen him. 'Come and meet Robin.'

Carlos forced himself to remain calm as he approached the couple who were now embracing.

He'd like to punch lover boy's teeth out! How dared he touch Sarah like that? His Sarah! The girl he'd been planning to marry before this inconsiderate, irresponsible rascal turned up.

'Robin, this is Carlos. The dear friend who helped me get this job. I told you about him, didn't I? We've known each other…well, for ever.'

Carlos gritted his teeth as he heard Sarah give a girly sort of laugh. She seemed to have recovered from her attack of nerves and appeared to be enjoying this reunion with the father of her child. He loathed the way she'd described him as being a 'dear friend'.

Looking at the pair of them now, chatting amiably, he couldn't think why Sarah had wanted him to be there. She was coping extremely well. Too well! In fact, she was giving her estranged lover too much attention for his liking.

Robin was stretching out his arm towards Carlos. The two men shook hands.

'Sarah tells me you're working in Africa, Robin.'

'Yes. I managed to get a couple of weeks off so I could get over to Rome to see Sarah. I told my boss that my girlfriend was expecting a baby and I needed time off to make sure she was OK.'

Carlos took a deep breath. 'So why didn't you phone Sarah to say you were coming?'

Robin looked down at his feet, shifting them uneasily on the tiled floor.

'I've been pretty busy since our last phone conversation. Most of the time I've been out in the bush, checking on patients who can't get to our medical centre. It's a tough job but somebody's got to do it. I wasn't sure until the last minute that I'd be able to get some time off.'

Robin raised his eyes and stared Carlos in the face as if defying him to make any more veiled insinuations of neglect. Deliberately, with studied nonchalance, Robin put his arm around Sarah and drew her towards him with a possessive gesture.

'You see, Carlos, with a difficult job like mine, you don't have too much time to think about your personal life. When Sarah first phoned me to say she was expecting my baby I was pretty confused, I can tell you. But over the months it's become clearer. I know exactly what I have to do.'

Carlos took a step forward, his hands clenched tightly by his sides. 'Well, having taken a long time to come to a decision, I hope you're making the right one.'

Sarah tried to move away from Robin but found her shoulders held in a possessive, vice-like grip. Not wanting to create a scene between the two men, she remained absolutely still.

'Oh, yes, I've thought everything through,' Robin said evenly. 'I took my time but I knew Sarah would be well looked after. I mean, actually being on the staff of a first-class, streamlined hospital like this…' He broke off as he looked around him. 'Fantastic place you've got here, Carlos! What's it like, working here?'

Carlos knew that Robin was trying to excuse his negligent behaviour by changing the subject. He drew himself to his full height so that he could look down on Robin with a proud, haughty stare. It wasn't worth becoming too antagonistic but he wasn't going to be won over by unimportant conversation.

'We have all taken great care of Sarah since she discov-red she was pregnant,' Carlos said, with steely calm. Now, if you will excuse me, I have to get back to my work. I'm going away tomorrow to a conference in Milano for a couple of weeks so—'

'Carlos, you've been working all day,' Sarah said, putting out her hand to detain him. 'Can't you delegate your work for this evening? We could all go out for a meal somewhere.'

'Much better for the two of you to talk things over together by yourselves,' Carlos said. 'You've got a lot to talk about.'

As he turned and headed for Pronto Soccorso he could feel his stomach churning. He'd taken an instant dislike to Robin, the man who had a claim on everything he held dear. Robin didn't love Sarah as he did. He'd totally ignored her in the early months when she'd needed support. But now here he was, and from the confident, possessive way he was behaving, that could only mean one thing.

Robin had taken his time in contemplating the idea of fatherhood but he was now ready to make a commitment to the mother of his child.

CHAPTER NINE

As soon as Sarah awoke next morning, she tried to phone Carlos. On both his room phone and his mobile the answering-machine clicked in. She was asked to leave a message. She hesitated. Carlos must have set off for Milan already. He wouldn't want her bothering him with her problems. She knew he'd got to give an important lecture this afternoon. The last thing he needed was Sarah to worry him about her problems.

She hung up and leaned back against her pillows. She'd wanted to discuss what Robin had said to her last night. Or, rather, what he hadn't said! He'd always been a vague sort of person. She'd never quite got to know how his mind worked even when they'd lived together for almost a year. So often Robin would say one thing and mean another.

So, after a couple of hours in a noisy *trattoria* with Robin last night, Sarah really didn't have a clue how Robin viewed his future as a father. What's more, she didn't think he had a clue either! She had the impression he'd simply been stringing her along, sounding her out as to whether she needed him full time, part time or not at all.

At the end of the meal, over coffee, she'd made it very clear that she was happy to be a single mother. She'd also told Robin about how supportive Carlos had been.

'Exactly how supportive?' Robin had asked.

Annoyingly, she'd felt herself blushing. 'Well…'

Robin had looked surprised. 'That supportive! I see.'

It had been at that point that Sarah had suggested they adjourn their discussion for the evening. She'd felt too tired to continue. Possibly Robin would like to phone her and

160

make it clear exactly how much involvement he wanted then they would be able to reach a mutual agreement.

But this morning, as she climbed out of bed and began getting ready for work, she felt apprehensive about the outcome of any further discussions. Robin had booked himself into a hotel for the next two weeks. Why on earth did he need two weeks in Rome? It was particularly difficult because Carlos would be in Milan.

She prayed that, despite the familiar, proprietorial way that Robin had behaved last night, he was not harbouring nostalgic ideas about getting back together again.

Arriving in Pronto Soccorso, she was met by Vittorio Vincenzi. He informed her that Carlos had left instructions that Sarah should only work until lunchtime each day for the next two weeks, after which she would be taking maternity leave.

Feeling tired after her wearying evening with Robin, she was relieved that Carlos had found time to rearrange the duty roster. This morning she was scheduled to deal with minor emergencies as and when they arrived in the department.

Her first patient was a little boy with a nosebleed. His nose had to be plugged with gauze before the bleeding stopped. Sarah did a variety of tests to make sure he wasn't suffering from anything serious before she was able to reassure the parents that their son had simply banged his nose too hard when he'd fallen off the swing.

Having cleaned up her patient after she'd plugged his nose, Sarah inserted a couple of stitches in the cut below his lip. Soon afterwards, satisfied that there was no further bleeding, she removed the plug and told the parents they could take their little boy home.

After treating several simple fractures and a man who

needed sutures after cutting his hand on a bottle, Sarah was surprised to find that it was almost lunchtime.

Going outside, she checked the messages on her mobile. Nothing from Carlos, but Robin had left a message asking her to meet him as soon as she was free. He wanted her to show him round some of the main tourist sites of Rome. She groaned. What she needed was a definite answer to her question. How much did he want to be involved as a father?

She decided she would arrange to meet him so that she could try to get him to make a decision this afternoon. He really was the most infuriating, vacillating man she'd ever had the misfortune to become involved with!

By the end of Robin's first week in Rome, Sarah's patience was wearing decidedly thin. She was also feeling sad that Carlos hadn't phoned her. He'd been at the conference for a whole week and she hadn't heard from him. During her afternoons off duty, she'd toured around Rome with Robin until she'd begun to think she wouldn't be able to look at another ancient monument, church or museum in her life.

But the wretched man still hadn't put his cards on the table. It was definitely showdown time! She'd been very patient, but she couldn't waste any more time on him. He may be the father of her child but she felt she owed him nothing more.

'Look, Robin, my feet are killing me, my back's aching and I'd like to go back to my room in the hospital,' she said, as she put out her hand to hail a passing cab. 'I'll drop you off at your hotel. We can talk in the cab...when I can attract the attention of one...'

They were walking away from the Colosseum. The noisy, honking cars seemed to be going every which way. All the cabs were occupied already. Suddenly one ground to a halt next to them. Sarah grabbed the handle and climbed in, moving her bulk with difficulty along the back seat so that there was room for Robin. The hot July afternoon was humid. Her skin, concealed beneath the cotton maternity dress she'd begun to hate, felt damp and sticky. What she needed was a cooling shower, a glass of cold water and Robin to go away and leave her in peace.

'Sarah, are you OK?'

'No, I'm not OK!'

The cab driver raised his head to look in his rear-view mirror at the heavily pregnant woman who was clearly distressed about something. Her husband seemed to be calming her down. As long as she didn't start giving birth in his newly cleaned cab! She'd asked to be taken to the Ospedale Tevere so he'd better get through this traffic as quickly as he could. Putting his hand firmly on the hooter, he pressed his foot down on the accelerator.

'Robin, I don't know why you came all this way to see me. You could have said everything you've said during the last few days over the phone.'

'But I wanted to make sure you were really OK, Sarah. You always say you're fine even when you're dropping in your tracks. It's my duty to give you my support. As a doctor I've seen so many pregnant women whose partners gave them little or no support.'

'Robin, doing the dutiful thing isn't what I want at all! It isn't what I really need, and I understand you well enough to know that you'd soon get tired of being dutiful. So, please, get rid of your guilt complex. It doesn't suit you.'

She took a deep breath before continuing. 'I know you may find it difficult to believe but I'm actually with Carlos. I love him very much. The day you arrived he'd asked me to move into his apartment. But your arrival complicated everything because—'

She had to break off as she clung, breathlessly, to the edge of her seat while the taxi hurtled round a bend.

She tried again. 'You see, the problem is that Carlos has always worried that you might want to take full responsibility for your child and—'

'Sarah, I didn't want to come here! I only came to Rome because my girlfriend made me come!'

'Your girlfriend? You didn't say…'

Robin leaned towards her. 'I didn't want to tell you about her because I thought you might be upset as you're carrying my child. Celine is a French nursing sister. We're very much in love. I think this might be the real thing. We started discussing the idea that we might get married. I felt I had to come clean and tell her about you and the baby. Believe it or not, you were on my conscience even before Celine pointed out where my duty lay.'

'I've never thought of you as having a conscience, Robin,' Sarah said evenly.

'Oh, yes! I've been feeling really guilty. Sarah, I'm really sorry I came round to the flat and got you into bed. I should have gone to that party. I should have—'

'Oh, Robin! It's no good worrying about what happened. That's not going to solve anything!'

Sarah leaned back against the seat, letting out a deep sigh as the memories of that fateful evening flooded back.

'Sarah, I'm really sorry you fell pregnant. There you were, having a nice quiet evening, and I turned up and started pouring champagne and—'

'Robin, let's forget that evening, shall we?' Sarah said quickly.

Robin nodded. 'You know, Sarah, when I talked over my problems about you and the baby with Celine, she became really concerned. She pointed out that my first duty was to you and the baby. She said she couldn't marry me if you were in need of my support.'

Sarah gave a slow smile as she realised the truth about Robin's mercy mission to Rome.

'It sounds like you've got a really nice girlfriend. She's obviously having a good influence on you.' She hesitated. 'Somehow I didn't think you could have changed all that much.'

Robin gave a sheepish grin. 'I've changed enough to agree to marriage, but I hope Celine and I will have a few years as a couple before the kids start arriving… What I mean is…'

'Don't worry, I know what you mean, Robin. I know you're not keen on being a father right now. So you wouldn't mind if you only saw our daughter occasionally, would you?'

'Well, I'd like to keep in touch with both of you,' he said carefully. 'Maybe when Charlotte grows up a bit she could… Well, perhaps not. Sarah, I'm always on the move in my new job. Travelling and babies don't really mix, do they?'

'Not really.' Sarah folded her hands over her bump, hoping that Charlie wasn't taking any of this personally. 'Robin, I really think you should marry your lovely girlfriend as soon as possible. I'll give you a progress report on Charlotte now and again and I'll put your name on the birth certificate as the biological father. But you won't mind if Carlos takes over your paternal duties, will you?'

'Of course I won't,' Robin said quickly, unable to disguise the relief he was feeling now that his ordeal was over. 'If you two get married and Carlos wants to adopt Charlotte, I'll be more than happy to sign any legal document that's required.'

'I'll remember that.'

Having done his duty, Robin was staring out of the window now. 'Oh, look, We're nearly at my hotel.'

Thank God! Sarah thought.

Robin tried to tell the driver that he wanted to be dropped

off. The driver didn't seem to understand so Sarah leaned forward.

'*Fermi qui, per favore!* Stop here, please!'

The taxi ground to a halt.

'Thanks, Sarah.' Robin climbed out. He was still holding onto the door as he turned back to look at her. 'I'll probably cut short my visit and go back to Africa as soon as I can get a flight. Doesn't seem much point in staying in Rome now that I can assure my girlfriend you really don't need me.'

'I agree.' She was feeling better already! '*Buon viaggio!*'

'What does that mean?'

'Have a good journey!' And the sooner the better!

Robin waved from the pavement. Sarah thought he hadn't looked so happy since he'd first arrived in Rome!

The cab driver was completely mystified. 'Shall I drive on to the hospital now?'

Sarah smiled as she leaned happily against the back of the seat. 'Yes, please. I work there.'

The driver let in his clutch and drove at a slower speed. He'd misjudged the situation. His passenger wasn't about to give birth after all. And what about the young man who'd just climbed out, leaving the lady to pay the bill? Who was he?

He knew he'd never be able to understand the strange ways of the English!

'Carlos! I'm phoning to see how things are going for you at the conference.'

As soon as she'd got back to her room, elated by the outcome of her discussion with Robin, Sarah had picked up the phone and called Carlos. Now she stretched out on the bed, kicking off her shoes as she sipped the cold glass of water she'd been longing for all afternoon. Ah, that was better! Her spirits lifted even further at the sound of Carlos's voice.

'Sarah, you're lucky to catch me. My mobile is switched off during the day when I'm in the lecture hall. He sounded breathless. 'I haven't had a minute to spare. I'm between lectures at the moment. I haven't phoned you because I thought you and Robin needed time to consider what you were going to do.'

'Well, I've spent a lot of time taking Robin around Rome and—'

'Why? I thought Robin was here to discuss your future.'

'He is, or rather he was. He's going to go back to Africa now that everything is decided.'

She heard Carlos drawing his breath.

'So what have you decided?' he asked, evenly.

'Robin wants minimal contact with Charlotte and me, so—'

'You told me that before. But I'm not convinced. If Robin wants to claim—'

'Robin doesn't want to claim anything.'

'Once the baby is born he'll want to take over.'

'He won't! He—'

'Sorry, Sarah, I've got to go back into the lecture room. We'll carry on this conversation when I get back next week. It's no use discussing something as important as this over the phone. Tell me how you're feeling. You're still OK, aren't you? Not too tired?'

'I'm fine, but, Carlos, about Robin—'

'Sorry, I'm being paged. I'll have to switch off my mobile and go back into the hall. We'll talk when I get back.'

She stared down at her phone, wondering how she was going to get through the next week. Carlos, oh, Carlos! Why did you have to go away just when I really need you?

It was the longest week of her life but somehow she managed to struggle through it. In one way it helped that she was busy at work during the mornings. She was so tired in the afternoons that she lay down on her bed and slept. Her body felt so heavy and there was a dragging feeling in her lower abdomen.

Halfway through the week she went to see Alessandro. He gave her a scan and a full examination before assuring her there was nothing to worry about. As she was nearly thirty-two weeks pregnant, he said he was relieved that she was to go on maternity leave in a few days' time. He suggested she take the rest of the week off, but Sarah said she preferred to finish her work.

As she left Alessandro's consulting room she'd told herself that the busier she was, the shorter the time would seem before Carlos came back. And preparing for her party at the end of the week would keep her mind off her problems.

Helena had been a tower of strength, helping Sarah to organise her combined leaving and birthday party, which was scheduled to take place at the end of her final day. One of the larger treatment rooms which was standing empty, waiting to be renovated, had been appropriated and all the regular medical staff in Pronto Soccorso had been invited.

Sarah had been in touch with the kitchen and arranged for a simple buffet to be laid out in the evening. The medical staff who were still on duty would come in for a drink and a snack whenever they could get away.

Her birthday coincided with her last morning on duty. As the morning session ended, Sarah went along to the party room to check that everything was organised for the party later on. Some of the doctors and nurses had hung streamers and balloons from the ceiling. Three trestle tables, covered in old sheets, were ready for the party snacks the kitchen staff would deliver later in the afternoon. A couple of old redundant examination couches had been placed against the wall. They would be useful for anyone who needed to sit down—like herself!

She reflected that her thirtieth birthday had been pretty uneventful so far. A few cards had arrived in the post, but it was tonight when the real celebration would start.

Lucy was going to arrive in a couple of hours. And Carlos would be here this evening, although she didn't know what time.

It was difficult to contain her excitement! She put a hand over her abdomen. Charlotte had been kicking wildly this morning during the time that she'd been at her busiest. Her baby seemed to have moved into a most uncomfortable position, very low down, almost as if she was getting ready to... Oh, no! She'd got another two months to go. Eight weeks of getting bigger and carrying a kicking Charlotte around!

As Sarah left the party room and walked along the corridor towards the canteen, she was aware that her back was aching again. She needed a light lunch, followed by as long a rest as there was time for.

'Lucy, where are you?' Sarah sat up on her bed, clutching her mobile as she listened to her sister's voice telling her that she'd just checked into her hotel. She'd been in the middle of a deep sleep but she was wide awake now. 'You won't be late for our party, will you?'

'Our party?'

Sarah smiled. 'Of course it's our party. Since when have we ever had separate birthdays?'

'But I haven't helped you with any of the arrangements, Sarah. Do you need any help now?'

'It's all organised. Just come along to A and E this evening. The staff will show you which room the party's in. Happy birthday, Lucy!'

'Happy birthday Sarah!'

Putting down the phone, she reflected that there had been no word from Carlos today. Maybe he'd forgotten it was her birthday. Maybe he wasn't going to make it to her birthday party.

As she climbed off her bed she realised that her backache hadn't gone away. Well, tomorrow she wouldn't have to get up for work. She could have a long lie-in and get herself fit again. That's all she needed. A good rest.

But you've just been resting all afternoon, said a tiny nagging voice at the back of her mind. Don't you think it would be wise to go and be checked out? She put a hand over her abdomen. Charlotte had stopped kicking. Yes, she did seem a bit low down…

'Charlie, if you're listening, don't do anything stupid to-night, like beginning to dive downwards, will you? You need another eight weeks inside Mummy's tummy to make you into a big strong girl. Tomorrow I'll go and see Alessandro again and see what you're up to but, in the meantime, just let Mummy have her birthday party in peace, will you?'

Sarah walked slowly into the room where the party was being held. The room led directly off the corridor, which meant that the party wouldn't cause any disruption in the main area of Pronto Soccorso. She'd agreed with Helena on the time she would arrive. Most of her off-duty colleagues were already there.

'*Buon compleanno!* Happy birthday, Sarah!' They were holding up their glasses in a toast. Sarah felt a lump in her throat.

'I'm going to miss you all,' she said. 'But I'll be back as soon as I can.'

Her friends were keen that she should open her presents, which had been laid out on one of the long trestle tables. They gathered around her while she tore off the wrapping paper, exclaiming with enthusiasm as each present was revealed.

'You're all so kind!'

Some of the presents were for her—bottles of scent, boxes of chocolates a couple of bottles of champagne to wet the baby's head. But the majority of items were for her baby. Dear little sleeping suits, bootees, a pink dress, some cuddly toys...

Sarah's eyes filled with tears as she thanked everybody. Turning round in the middle of her thank-you speech, she saw her sister coming through the door. The people nearest to Lucy did a double-take as they glanced at Sarah's double.

'Let me introduce my twin sister, Lucy,' Sarah said, moving slowly through the people standing around her.

The two sisters hugged. Everybody called out, '*Buon compleanno!* Happy birthday, Lucy!' Lucy smiled her acknowledgement.

Sarah stood back to look in admiration at her sister. 'Lucy, you look fabulous! Oh, will I ever be so slim again?'

She put her hands down over her abdomen as a particularly strong pang seemed to shoot through from the back to the front. Warning bells were sounding inside her head. She wasn't...she couldn't be...

She straightened up. The pain had gone. It was the excitement of the day and the anticipation of knowing that Carlos would be returning shortly.

The door was opening again, but the man coming in, carrying a large bouquet of flowers, wasn't Carlos.

'Robin!' she gasped. 'What are you doing here? I thought you'd gone back to Africa.'

Robin grinned. 'I couldn't change my flight so I decided to stay on and play at being a tourist for a bit longer. Then I remembered it was your birthday. We had a spectacularly awful time on your birthday last year, as I recall.'

In spite of the shock of seeing Robin again after she'd thought him safely in Africa, Sarah found herself smiling as the memory of last year's birthday flooded back.

'That was the evening when we both decided it was time to call it a day, wasn't it?'

Robin leaned forward and kissed her lightly on the cheek. 'It's good we can both laugh about it now. Happy birthday, Sarah!'

As Robin thrust the bouquet of flowers into her arms Sarah suddenly became aware that Carlos was standing in the doorway. Oh, no! How long had he been there? This little scene between the two of them might be misinterpreted.

He was looking so handsome in one of his well-cut summer-weight suits, making his way towards her. Their eyes met. She wanted to fling herself into his arms but his face held a cool, enigmatic expression.

'Good evening Robin,' he said haughtily. 'I thought you had gone back to Africa.'

'I couldn't change my flight,' Robin said, warily glancing from Sarah to Carlos. 'I called in briefly to wish Sarah a happy birthday.'

Carlos curled his lip. 'How thoughtful of you.'

'Welcome back, Carlos.'

Helena, circulating the room with a tray of drinks, stopped to hand her boss a glass of champagne. She turned to look at Robin. 'Champagne?'

Robin lifted his glass towards Sarah. 'Happy birthday!'

'*Buon compleanno*, Sarah!' Carlos said.

As Sarah looked at Carlos she felt a shiver of apprehension running through her. His eyes still held that strange expression. The warmth of their rapport simply wasn't there any more. If only Robin hadn't arrived and made it look as if he wanted to be a caring father! She had to convince

Carlos that Robin wasn't going to keep turning up out of the blue in the future.

Helena had put down her tray and joined their small group.

'Helena, this is Dr Robin Hardcastle, a friend from England,' Sarah said.

Helena smiled. 'I like to speak English to you.'

Robin looked relieved that some of the tension was easing with the arrival of Helena.

'Very impressive hospital you have here, Helena,' he said.

'You like I show you round hospital, Doctor?'

'I'd like that very much,' Robin said quickly. Anything to escape from Carlos Fellini!

'Carlos, we've got to talk,' Sarah began, as soon as Helena and Robin had disappeared.

'Not now, Sarah. Too many people around. And you look tired,' Carlos said as he sipped his drink.

'I was going to say the same about you.'

'It's been a difficult two weeks.'

She swallowed hard. 'Yes, it has.'

'It was very difficult to concentrate, knowing that you were with Robin.'

'Carlos, I wasn't with Robin, well, not in the sense that you're implying.'

'Carlos!' Lucy came across the room towards them. 'It's a long time since I saw you. You haven't changed a bit.'

Carlos smiled. 'Neither have you. We'll have time to catch up with each other when you start work here. Will you be able to work tomorrow? With Sarah going off on maternity leave...'

Sarah moved away. She felt heavy and useless. And a bit apprehensive. She wasn't in a party mood any more. She found herself going through the motions of being sociable but she was longing to be alone again. Alone with Carlos…if he wanted to be alone with her.

She poured herself another glass of water and put on her plastic smile. Not long now! Carlos was circulating, the centre of attention in whichever group he joined. Colleagues who were still on duty rushed in occasionally, had a quick drink of the non-alcoholic punch that Sarah had prepared, wished her a happy birthday and went back to work again.

One by one her guests began to drift away. Lucy had excused herself early, saying she needed to get some sleep before starting her new job in the morning.

At last they were alone, just Carlos and herself. Carlos was at the other side of the room, gathering up the empty bottles. Sarah found a bin liner and began to stuff the plastic plates inside it.

She looked across the room at Carlos. 'Carlos, please, leave that. Will you come over here? We need to talk.'

He moved towards her, looking down at her solemnly.

'Robin's been gone a long time,' he said. 'Is he going to come back here?'

'Carlos, I don't know!' She turned quickly from him and as she moved away she felt an excruciating pain.

'Aagh!'

She felt herself collapsing against Carlos as the deep pain whipped through her abdomen.

'Sarah, darling, what's the matter? Oh, no, not yet. You can't be…'

Carlos was supporting her towards the examination couch at the side of the wall. Pushing away the plastic cups and plates that littered the surface, he cradled her firmly in his arms before lowering her onto the couch.

'Tell me exactly what that pain felt like, Sarah.'

She groaned. 'I hate to admit it but I think I'm going into premature labour. I've been feeling a bit weird all day

And tonight my backache has been getting worse. I… Oh, Carlos!'

'Let me check what's happening,' Carlos said as he flipped back Sarah's voluminous cotton skirt. 'Maybe it's not too late to prevent you going into premature labour.'

He broke off as he checked the birth canal. The cervix was fully dilated. He could already see the top of the baby's head. Charlotte's head was crowning!

'What's the matter, Carlos? There's something wrong, isn't there? Tell me what—Aagh!'

Carlos took hold of the crown of the head and gently eased its passage through the cervix. As the uterine contraction finished he reassessed the situation. There was a further complication. The umbilical cord was around the baby's neck. He felt a shiver of fear running through him.

He'd had to deal with this complication several times in his professional career and he'd coped with calm and expertise. But this was Sarah, his precious Sarah, and the slimy, blood-covered, red-faced, angry-looking head he was holding in his hands belonged to Charlotte, his precious Charlotte!

'Don't push, Sarah. For God's sake, don't push until I tell you to. Pant if you feel you want to push, but—'

'I want to push,' Sarah screamed, before beginning to pant as she'd been told. 'What's happening?'

'I'm trying to remove the cord from around Charlotte's neck…'

Carlos slipped a finger under the pubic arch as he attempted to place the cord where it wouldn't tighten around the baby's neck and strangle her.

Sarah moaned. 'OK…I…understand. I…'

'I've done it, Sarah! The cord's free. You can push on the next… That's fine… I've got the body in my hands… The legs are coming now… Oh, Sarah…'

There was a thin wail of protest as Carlos placed the slimy, squalling infant on Sarah's abdomen.

'Is everything OK in here?'

Night Sister walked in through the door. 'I thought I heard... Oh, my God. Why have you brought a patient in here, Carlos?'

Carlos gave a relieved smile. 'Because it's her birthday, Sister. And we've just added another birthday.'

He wiped the sweat from his forehead with the back of his hand. 'Would you mind getting me some sterile scissors so I can cut the cord, Sister? I'll also need an incubator and a dressing sheet. And will you alert Obstetrics, please? Tell them there's an eight-week premature baby and her mother requiring full postnatal checks and treatment.'

As soon as Carlos was able to cut the cord, he wrapped Charlotte in a dressing sheet and handed her to Sarah.

He put his arm around Sarah's shoulders as she cuddled Charlotte.

'She's so tiny, Carlos!'

'She seems amazingly healthy for a thirty-two-week gestation baby. We'll need to check her lungs. She's breathing OK at the moment but... Ah, here comes the incubator... And, Alessandro, how nice of you to drop in.'

'Where were you, Alessandro? I invited you to my birthday party,' Sarah said, still cuddling her baby, unable to believe that Charlotte had actually arrived.

Alessandro strode across the room. 'I've only just got out of Theatre,' he told Charlotte in English. 'Still, better late than never. I have to say that this is totally unexpected, Sarah. Let's have a look at this impatient baby...Charlotte, isn't it? I remember that was the name you told me you'd given her. Well, she looks very healthy for a prem. I'll take you both along to obstetrics so we can check up on the pair of you.'

He turned to look at Carlos. 'And the proud father will be coming along as well, I presume?'

'Alessandro, I'll be coming along, but you know perfectly well that I'm not the biological father.'

Alessandro smiled at his colleague. 'According to Sarah, you're already more of a father to Charlotte than the biological father will ever be.'

He stretched out his hand towards Carlos. 'Congratulations, *papà*!'

The door burst open as Robin rushed in.

'Sarah, oh, Sarah, I've just heard. You poor darling, going into premature labour like that... Oh, but what an adorable baby! I'd like to hold her... Don't worry, everybody, I've delivered a few babies in my time. I won't drop her. And I know she's got to go into the incubator, but her breathing is OK at the moment...'

Sarah allowed Robin to take Charlotte into his arms.

Robin cradled the tiny child against him. 'Sarah, she's gorgeous! Of all the babies I've ever seen, this one is the most beautiful little treasure in the world, aren't you, my darling?'

Alessandro was frowning. 'Would someone like to introduce me to this...er...gentleman?' he asked in impeccable, distinct English.

'This is Dr Robin Hardcastle,' Carlos said evenly. 'Charlotte's biological father.'

CHAPTER TEN

CARLOS hurried along the corridor, crossing over from the hospital to the medical residents' quarters. He was keeping his head down. He didn't want to meet anybody he knew. He wanted to reach the sanctuary of his room so that if his turbulent emotions erupted he could weep in private.

Seeing Robin holding his child, exclaiming how beautiful she was, had been everything he'd feared would happen. He remembered how moved he'd been when he'd watched the final act of *Madame Butterfly* with Sarah. The father returning to claim his child! It was all too similar for him to bear. He could hear the poignant music in his head now. Shades of the operatic tragedy were haunting him...

He increased his pace, reaching for his keys. He pushed open his door, slamming it behind him as he strode across the room. His phone was ringing. He should leave it. But when had he ever left his phone to ring when it could be he was needed?

'Carlos?'

He took a deep breath as he felt his pulses quickening.

'Yes, Sarah,' he said quietly.

'Alessandro and his obstetrics team have finished my postnatal checks. Charlotte is in her incubator and Robin is just leaving so—'

'Robin is leaving? But I thought—'

'Carlos, Robin would like to see you before he goes. Could you come to Obstetrics?'

He swallowed hard. His mind was in turmoil now. Robin was leaving! But why? Unless...!

'I'm coming now!'

* * *

Sarah was sitting up in bed in her room in the obstetrics unit. Robin was standing beside her bed. When Carlos arrived Robin moved towards the door as if anxious to leave.

'I've got to go now, Carlos,' he said nervously. 'Early start for my plane in the morning. I just wanted to set the record straight. Seeing my baby tonight was a one-off experience. I know, in my heart of hearts, I can't be the father he deserves. As far as babies are concerned, I don't mind delivering them, but a lifetime commitment...'

'What are you trying to say, Robin?' Carlos said firmly, taking charge of the delicate situation.

Robin cleared his throat. 'I'm trying to say that I think you'd make a much better father to Charlotte than I would. And Sarah would be much happier with you than she ever was with me. Sarah tells me you've already bonded with Charlotte so if you feel you would like to adopt her I'll sign the required legal documents.'

Carlos felt as if he'd died and gone to heaven! Everything he'd hoped and prayed for was coming true. He gave a deep sigh of relief as he held out his hand towards Robin.

'That would make me very happy!' He hesitated. It had to be said. 'You're absolutely sure you won't change your mind, Robin?'

'No. It's the right thing to do. Thank you, Carlos.'

'Thank you, Robin.'

The two men shook hands.

Carlos smiled happily. He now knew exactly how he wanted this exceptional day to end.

'Robin, if you wouldn't mind staying with Sarah for one moment, I need to speak to Sister. Excuse me.'

Carlos stepped out into the corridor and hurried towards the obstetrics sister's room. Sister smiled and nodded her assent as Carlos made his unusual request. After a few brief words of thanks, he returned to find that Robin was waiting by the door, anxious to leave.

'Thank you, Robin,' Carlos said as he strode over to Sarah's bedside. 'I had to check on Sarah's treatment.'

Robin turned briefly at the door. 'Goodbye, Sarah.'

'Goodbye, Robin.'

As Carlos drew Sarah into his arms he knew he was the happiest man in the world. From the nightmare scenario of the early part of this evening, all his dreams had now come true!

'So Robin finally came to a decision!' he said.

Sarah snuggled against him. 'I tried to tell you last week on the phone but you were too busy to listen.'

'I'm sorry. I wouldn't have believed you over the phone anyway. I had to hear it from the man himself. How anybody could bear to leave…'

He lowered his head, his lips seeking hers as she clung to him. Their embrace was gentle at first and then surprisingly sensual considering the ordeal they'd been through…

Sarah raised her head and smiled. 'Mmm…I enjoyed that! Carlos, I haven't yet thanked you for delivering my baby.'

'Our baby!'

'That goes without saying now. You were wonderful!'

'So were you! I've never had a better patient. No painkillers, no technical intervention. Well, you said you wanted the birth to be as natural as possible. They don't come much more natural than that!'

Sarah was feeling tired but, oh, so happy. She was clean again, having been helped into her *en suite* shower room to have a quick shower. Behind her ears, she'd dabbed some of the expensive scent that Carlos had bought her before he'd left for Milan. Charlotte was spending the night in the premature baby unit, breathing easily in an incubator. The staff were well qualified and experienced with pre-nature babies so Sarah wasn't worried at being parted so soon from her precious baby.

She smiled. 'That's what Alessandro said when he checked me out. He said I was a natural mother.'

Carlos nodded. 'He told me that. But he told me that you're probably one of those patients who have very little warning that their labour has started. You've got a high pain threshold, so you're likely to have precipitous births. We'll have to remember that for next time.'

Sarah looked up. 'What next time?'

Carlos smiled. 'What is it you say in English? I'm putting the cart before the horse? Let me start again.'

He went down on one knee at the side of the bed. 'Sarah, will you marry me?'

She leaned forward, putting out her hand to clasp his. 'Of course I will. Oh, Carlos, I love you so much. Please, get up and hold me. I want to show you just how much I've missed you.'

Carlos's kiss silenced her. She felt a tremor of excitement running through her. She'd been surprised at how sexy she'd felt towards Carlos during her pregnancy but she hadn't been prepared for the deep desire she felt in her postnatal state!

'We'll get married as soon as we can,' Carlos whispered huskily.

'Let's leave it about six weeks. Then we can be sure it's safe to make love.'

Carlos raised one eyebrow. 'Six weeks?'

Sarah smiled. 'I think that in my case, as I didn't have any stitches, I'll probably use my own discretion. I feel ready to make love now but—No, Carlos!'

She laughed as Carlos pretended to climb onto the bed. 'We'll have to be patient.'

Carlos gave her a rakish grin. 'Well, you're the medical expert in this case, *Dottore*. You have inside information

on the patient. You can ask Alessandro for his advice when
he gives you an internal examination.'

'Alessandro told me he usually recommends six weeks
before marital relations are resumed.' She smiled. 'But I'm
probably a special case as I didn't have to go the full nine
months. 'He also thinks that Charlotte will be ready to go
home as soon as she's gained enough weight.'

'We'll have to decide where we want to live, Sarah. Will
you really be happy in the Rome apartment?'

'Of course I will! It's a beautiful apartment.'

'Then there are the two houses at the coast. My parents
have gone back to live in the house next door to the Villa
Florissa. But the Villa Florissa, the one you stayed in as a
child, the one we slept in on the night of *Madame Butterfly*,
is still empty. They've asked me if I'd like to take over
that one. My mother says that looking after one house at
her age is more than enough.'

'Are you planning to rent it out again?'

Carlos drew her closer into the circle of his arms, leaning
his head against hers. 'The house belongs to both of us
now, Signora Fellini, as does the apartment in Rome. So,
what do you think we should do with the house down at
the coast?'

Sarah turned her head to look up at Carlos. 'I think we
should spend our honeymoon there with baby Charlotte.
After that, we can use it as a weekend house. Then, when
the family has grown larger and I'm a full-time mother…'

'I think you are a full-time mother already, Sarah,'
Carlos said, caressing her cheek lovingly. 'You mustn't
think about going back to work for a long time. Why not
wait until our family has grown up, perhaps when the children are in college?'

Sarah smiled. 'I can safely leave that decision for a
while. First I've got a wedding to plan. When I tell my

amily, they'll probably want us to get married at our vil-
age church. How would you feel about that, Carlos?'

He kissed her gently on the lips, his kiss deepening be-
ore he pulled himself away and smiled lovingly into her
yes.

'I don't mind where we're married so long as it's actually
oing to happen. I still can't believe that it's all turned out
o well.'

'Neither can I. Do you remember when we were at the
revi Fountain? My secret wish was that nothing would
revent us being together. My wish came true.'

'My wish was very similar after we'd thrown three coins
n the fountain.'

He swallowed hard as the poignant memories flooded
ack.

'Carlos, I wish you didn't have to leave me tonight.'

'Close your eyes and wish, my love! Perhaps if you wish
ard enough I might be able to stay.'

'What do you mean?'

The double doors to Sarah's room were opening. A por-
er was pushing a bed through.

'Magic!' Carlos said, his mouth twitching.

Sarah laughed. 'When did you arrange this, Carlos?'

'I told you it was magic! Your wish is my command.'

The porter pushed the bed against the wall. 'It was you
hat ordered this bed wasn't it, Dr Fellini?'

Carlos pretended to look surprised. 'I suppose I must
ave done. Well, thank you, Luigi. That was perfect timing.
You can leave the bed there. I'll find a use for it.'

The door closed behind the porter. Carlos drew Sarah
gainst him.

'I'm going to go and say goodnight to our precious
aughter now. Any message?'

Sarah smiled. 'Just tell Charlotte I love her and I'm longing to hold her again…almost as much as I'm longing to hold you, Carlos.'

'I'll be back soon.'

'I'll be waiting for you…'

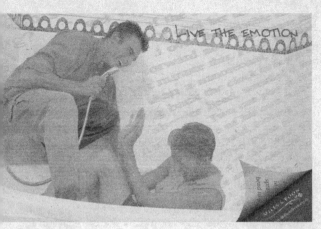

Modern
romance™

...international affairs
- seduction and
passion guaranteed

Tender
romance™

...sparkling, emotional,
feel-good romance

Historical
romance™

...rich, vivid and
passionate

Medical
romance™

...pulse-raising
romance – heart-
racing medical drama

Sensual
romance™

...teasing, tempting,
provocatively playful

Blaze™

...scorching hot
sexy reads

27 new titles every month.

Live the emotion

MILLS & BOON®

MB5

MILLS & BOON®

Live the emotion

_Medical
romance™

0704/03b

EMERGENCY: BACHELOR DOCTOR
by Gill Sanderson   (Special Care Baby Unit)

On her first day at the Wolds Hospital, Dr Kim Hunter was not expecting to work in the Special Care Baby Unit – and neither was she expecting the impact that her new colleague, Dr Harry Black, had on her! Kim found herself falling for him, and then discovered the heartbreaking reasons behind his fear of commitment…

RAPID RESPONSE by Jennifer Taylor

(A&E Drama)

Two years ago Holly Daniels's fiancé walked out without warning – and now the two specialist registrars are reunited, forced to work side by side in the Rapid Response team of a busy emergency unit. Holly's surprised at how fast her heart reacts to Ben Carlisle, and Ben is just as quick to react – so why did he walk away in the first place…?

DOCTORS IN PARADISE by Meredith Webber

Tranquillity Sands is a health resort set on a coral-fringed island surrounded by the Pacific – what could possibly go wrong in this perfect place? Everything, as far as Dr Caroline Sayers is concerned! She finds herself in the midst of intrigue, superstition and medical emergency – and through it all strolls Dr Lucas Quinn: laid-back, caring…and utterly irresistible!

On sale 6th August 2004

Available at most branches of WHSmith, Tesco, Martins, Borders, Eason, Sainsbury's and all good paperback bookshops.

MILLS & BOON®

Volume 2
on sale from
6th August
2004

Lynne
GRAHAM

International Playboys

A Savage
Betrayal

Next month don't miss –

HOT SUMMER LOVING

Sit back and enjoy the sun with these sizzling summer stories. They're hot, passionate and irresistibly sexy!

On sale 6th August 2004

Available at most branches of WHSmith, Tesco, Martins, Borders, Eason, Sainsbury's and all good paperback bookshops.

0704/05

4 FREE

books and a surprise gift!

We would like to take this opportunity to thank you for reading thi
Mills & Boon® book by offering you the chance to take FOUR
more specially selected titles from the Medical Romance™ serie
absolutely FREE! We're also making this offer to introduce you to
the benefits of the Reader Service™—

- ★ FREE home delivery
- ★ FREE gifts and competitions
- ★ FREE monthly Newsletter
- ★ Exclusive Reader Service offers
- ★ Books available before they're in the shops

Accepting these FREE books and gift places you under no
obligation to buy, you may cancel at any time, even after receiving
your free shipment. Simply complete your details below and return
the entire page to the address below. ***You don't even need a stamp!***

YES! Please send me 4 free Medical Romance books and a surprise
gift. I understand that unless you hear from me, I will receive
6 superb new titles every month for just £2.69 each, postage and
packing free. I am under no obligation to purchase any books and
may cancel my subscription at any time. The free books and gift will
be mine to keep in any case.

M4ZED

Ms/Mrs/Miss/Mr ....Initials.................................
                                         BLOCK CAPITALS PLEASE

Surname ....

Address ....

....

....Postcode...........................

Send this whole page to:
UK: FREEPOST CN81, Croydon, CR9 3WZ
EIRE: PO Box 4546, Kilcock, County Kildare (stamp required)